GENETIC KILLING FIELDS

CHRONICLES OF ALTERNATE EARTH

PART 1

PETER A. RODRIGUEZ

GENETIC KILLING FIELDS
CHRONICLES OF ALTERNATE EARTH PART 1

iUniverse books may be ordered through booksellers or by contacting:

iUniverse
1663 Liberty Drive
Bloomington, IN 47403
www.iuniverse.com
844-349-9409

*Because of the dynamic nature of the Internet, any web addresses or
links contained in this book may have changed since publication and
may no longer be valid. The views expressed in this work are solely those
of the author and do not necessarily reflect the views of the publisher,
and the publisher hereby disclaims any responsibility for them.*

*Any people depicted in stock imagery provided by Getty Images are
models, and such images are being used for illustrative purposes only.
Certain stock imagery © Getty Images.*

ISBN: 978-1-6632-3336-3 (sc)
ISBN: 978-1-6632-3337-0 (e)

Library of Congress Control Number: 2022903014

Print information available on the last page.

iUniverse rev. date: 03/02/2022

DEDICATION

This book is dedicated first to The Rodriguez/ Collazo and Jimenez/Rivera Family. They were on the front lines and had to experience with me firsthand my trials and tribulations. Secondly, to all those who overcame adversities in their lives. When others saw the need to be negative and pull you down about your aspirations and visions, you overcame and succeeded despite any odds. Lastly, to my military Veterans and Law Enforcement brothers and sisters who always had my six. They supported and defended me when my loved ones couldn't be there to do so.

ACKNOWLEDGMENT

Much appreciation goes to those who helped me create the ideas and use their creativity to build this world. The illustrator, April Fitzgerald, your amazing artwork, and concepts help give life to my imagination. Attn.Braunstein for allowing me to use pieces of your law dissertation. All the iUniverse members who guided me along this journey and helped make my creativity be the best it can be. And all other staff members of iUniverse who assisted in the development and production of my book.

P.A. Rodriguez
Alpha 3.14

"Life is ambiguous. There is no right or wrong. No such thing as evil or good. Only experiences, changing emotions, and perspectives. Everything is relative. We all have a purpose. A reason why what we do what we do and why we act the way we act. There is always a beginning, but where does it end. At what point does our perspective change. Perhaps age, tragedy, or empathy. Our existence and relationships take curious turns as time progresses. Friends become enemies, Enemies allies. Then everything seems to return to natural form. The names, faces, and reasons are different and change. But the story always is the same. The story will always be the same. Life is ambiguous." – Late Grand Owl Xavier

1

ÎNCEPTION

Grand Owl Boris-

"I WILL BE RECITING THIS NARRATIVE TO YOU AS BEST I COULD,
as best I can in my old age. For that is my designation, it is what
I was born to do. It is the only thing I am allowed to do. It's our
war cry, "We observe and report". That is, it. It is forbidden to
do anything else. Without judgement, remorse, happiness, or
any other emotion. For if we intervene in any affair, the penalty
is of the highest order, death. The same penalties apply to those
who interfere with our manuscripts. For that reason, few try
and even less succeed. I am referred to as the Grand Owl. I
am the overseer and final authority of my kind. I am the last
word. What I proclaim did happen. When you earn the highest
position in your species you lose your born name and adopt
a title. No one can take this from you except the reaper itself.
To receive this title, well, every breed has different rituals. My
memory dates back longer and more accurate than any other,
The Vampires decide theirs by seniority and age. The Lycans
have a more primitive and savage contest for leadership. It's
simple and direct. The most vicious and battle-ready, fight to
the death earn the right to lead. A waist of a good warrior in
my opinion. I mention those two groups to emphasize the fact
that they are the two major waring faction, sworn to kill the
other off. To understand why they keep fighting is futile, that
is not my job anyway. As I said, I am to observe and report.

Instead, I will begin as I remember it being told to me. Shortly after the "Great Experiment" as it's become to be known. I was born into the Lion pride. See, every species must breed and maintain the owls for inscription purposes. We are assigned to other factions to serve as diplomats and record events as they happen. Growing up before my first assignment I was schooled by my mentor. An owl strictly adhered to the facts and nothing else. His name was Grand Owl Boris. I was to follow his lead, learn and remember. He died inadvertently in the "war of the spies". Whether or not his information was accurate is not my concern. Curiosity is a curious thing. Knowledge is its only motivational drive.

And as some may agree, knowledge is a tool to abuse power. And power can be a destructive force. Curiosity will be our starting point. For all intents and purposes, curiosity is the genesis for this war. The "Great Experiment" was the product of a curious DNA scientist who decided he would try to splice and combine human genes with animals. Dr. P. Brocknor developed this procedure without the consent and knowledge of his superiors. He began with Pitbull terriers at the local animal shelters from counties overrun in what was Philadelphia and New Jersey. Because they were on the list to be euthanized, there were an abundance of them, and basically no-one cared about them. Due to their unwarranted violent reputation, they received a fate undeserving. Now where do you think this Dr. was able to acquire human species. Think about it. Where could you go to get human volunteers who were rejected by their loved ones, unable to protest such questionable practices, and never truly worry about these "situations" to be uncovered? That's correct! Abortion clinics. This "Doctor" would conduct his experiments with dogs from animal shelters and aborted fetus'. Disturbing to say the least. What's even more unsettling, is that he succeeded in making his first human/K-9 hybrid. Basically, a human with strong canine features. We refer to their clan as the "Terriers". Short for the Pitbull terriers and the genesis of their kind. It's just a general term for all dog/human hybrids. They are sworn allies to the Lycans being a DNA cousin of theirs, they come to the aid of the "Weres" whenever their services are required and for whatever reason. Their war cry is "Loyalty over life". A culture tested time and time again with few exceptions. Their loyalty is so renowned, those who dare to challenge it have preempted for a fight. After Dr. P. Brocknor and his corps of rogue genetic engineers found the secret to success, they decided to venture into other animals found in the shelter. Cats of course. The next species prevalent in unloved quantity. And as you would guess. The human feline species, happily, referred to as "Grimalkins" naturally hated the terriers. Eventually pledging themselves to the Vampires. The "Grims" war cry is, "Where there is one, there are many". Meaning, if you pick a fight with one, be prepared to fight with many more. As fate would have it, curiosity got the upper hand on humans, hypnotizing rouge DNA specialists to create all forms of human/animal off springs. Monkeys, bears, rodents, aquatic animals, and birds. I supposed I should thank these curiosities. For if it were not for them, I would have not been here telling you this history. Anyway, it came to a point, where the humans perfected the gene splicing so these hybrids could shape-shift from human to animal, and back again. Inevitably, they lost control of these new beings, and in a twist of fate, became their prey and were hunted themselves.

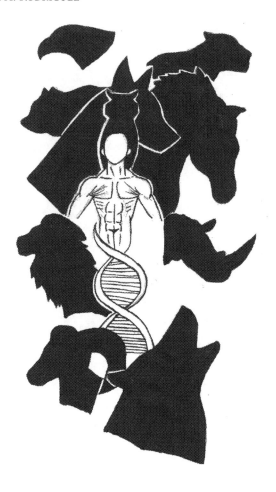

Enter the vampires. No one truly knows when, where, or how the Vamps came to be, but what we do know is that they are as old as humans themselves, living amongst them and feeding on the humans as needed. They live discreetly and very few humans even knew about their existence, until the Lycans decided they would eradicate their food source, the Humans. Another alternative rumor has it, that a pack of Lycans inadvertently fed on the yearly gathering of the toddlers from noble Vamp Clans. The last theory, which I tend to believe, is that the Vampires fight for the right to rule, and refuse to be subjugated by, in their view, a lesser and vile entity. Whichever the cause, this part of the ongoing saga, I'll start with a chase.

In a high grassland, a heavily vegetative terrain with marshy mud puddles, and ill-fated bushes designed to impede on traveled roads or paths. Sprints a lone greyhound terrier panting heavily, accompanied by fogs of breath. Is an information carrier. Designed just recon. If provoked and when necessary, he'll fight. He's quick and agile, but stamina is its main attribute. He's making an escape. An escape from those who would have his throat split open. You can hear the laughing and cackling not far behind. The sounds coming in six distinct tones but 2 different tempos. *"Fuckin hyenas and wild dogs"*, thinking to himself. Dustin, one of the last few of his k-9 breed. True to his kind and war cry. They had been chasing him from the Vamps war camp for miles. *"Just need to get to the sands"*, Dustin mumbled to himself. *"They dare not cross into a land where their own lives are at stake"*. Wild dogs and hyenas only fight when they feel they can win. The sand dunes, where the Komodo outnumber and patrol their territory, isn't a risk their willing to take. The Komodo are very predictable. Their war cry reinforces their behavior." We're neither friend nor foe". The heckling of the hyenas is unrelenting. You can hear them laughing at their own juvenile insults no matter how ridiculous they are." HEY GREYHOUND! WHY THE LONG FACE?". You can hear the others laughing and asking for more. "HEY GREY! DOES A RABBIT SHIT IN YOU FACE WHEN YOU'RE CHASING THEM?", clearly referring to their heritage of greyhound racing. *"Stupid ass Hyenas"*, Dustin thinks to himself, *"A few more miles."*. The message to Roderick is of the upmost importance. Information is crucial since the "War of the spies" left a lot of the raptors at a critical low and luxury to obtain. Until a wrong can be righted the great birds of prey have secluded themselves. Dustin's would be assailants, have come to believe that they would never catch him before he gets to the sandpits, so instead they prefer to shout out idol threats and insults. As the landscape changes from green to golden and dark to light, a sigh of relief comes over Dustin. He turns and yells "FUUCCKK YOOU!". One problem solved, makes room for another. The Komodo's deadly bite. Their only loyalty is to their mood, which changes by the second." *I must get across this stretch of sand if I'm going to get to my destination. PISS AND SHIT!"*, Dustin thinks to himself. A saying his mentor use to tell him whenever he was looking for sympathy. *"If you want sympathy from me, look on the ground under my piss and shit."*. Interesting thought. Several strides into the sands Dustin notices a dozen Komodo closing in on him. *"These fuckers waste no time looking for confrontation"*, he thought to himself. *"Damn IT! Red stripe painted between the eyes."*. They are the most vicious of their breed and is why they are designated soldiers. "You have about a heartbeat to explain to me why you are here! ", Demands the lead komodo. "I'm in route to deliver an important message to Roderick.", says Dustin. "Never heard of him," stated sarcastically by the lead Komodo. Dustin says, "One way or another, I'm crossing through this area.". The lead Komodo annoyed, dares Dustin, "Dead or dying. There's the line.". He immediately draws a line in the sand challenging Dustin to cross as others have and failed in the past. The lead Komodo grins in anticipation knowing the expected outcome if Dustin decides to accept the proposed offer. He takes a deep breath and says in his mind, *"Here we go."*

Dustin takes off weaving in and out of the snapping jaws of the Komodo not wasting time trying to fight a losing battle. Better to just outrun them. He gets by the first group untouched. As he crosses over the first sand dune, he realizes he has made a huge mistake. Thousands of these dragons bathing in the sand heat. They all turn to look at once. Dustin suddenly feels sickened inside his stomach, not because he is about to die, but he knows he's failed his mission to make it back west to the wolf's refuge and deliver a much urgent message.

Back at wolf's refuge, Roderick waits with his comrades on word from Dustin about his mission. Roderick asks, "Any word from Dustin or his greys?". "Not yet, we should have heard something by now.", answers Muscles. He is head of the Terrier species of K-9. Loyal to the cause and Roderick's Werewolves. Bronze who is also an ally, as well as leads the Stallions adds," Well, we all know what that means.". Roderick replies, "Absolutely! Strickland, Baxter ready your clans. Relay the order to the Rhinos. It's a go. Bronze and muscles you know what to do." Muscles both understand and carry out the order. They all leave except for one. Roderick turns to his trusted Captain and lover, Ruby. Named for her one eye that is blood red, similar to the rubies found only in the lands previously known as Israel. No one, not even Roderick knows what her other eye looks like because of the patch she wears constantly. She is almost as deadly and powerful as Roderick himself and he would not have it any other way. For the werewolves, strength and power is everything. Muscular in stature, she stands over six feet tall. Slightly bigger than the females of her kind. On her left hip, she carries a seven-inch sharpened blade used in close quarter combat. Ready to slice the neck of those who threaten her. A perfect match for Roderick. "If my calculations are correct, Dustin would have had to cross the sands to get here as quickly as possible, meaning…". Ruby interrupting," Meaning he ran into those fuckin Komodo and now, at some point, we're going to have to deal with them." Roderick agrees. "They have slighted us too many times. After these coming events, I'm sure Muscles is going to want to pay them a visit.". Ruby says, "He'll expect our loyalty to his cause when that time comes, just as much as his clan has shown to ours. Loyalty over life.". "And he'll have it, replies to Roderick. "Not only to secure his future fealty, and because these Komodo need to be taught respect."

Ruby adds, "Our fems are organizing the numbers for this fight. How young do you want to go?" Roderick pauses to think smartly. "Only those who have completed the suffering. Leave enough to train our future.", orders Roderick. Ruby asks, "What will you do until we're ready?". Answering Ruby's question, he says," Take a handful of our best and go talk to the Great Bears of spider stream. See if they'll join us. They have a stake in this fight as much as we do.". Ruby starts giggling at the notion. She reminds her lover that those bears of Spider stream, would rather remain fat and happy than to fight for a cause they don't believe in. She sarcastically wishes him good luck. Roderick gathers up everything needed for the journey, kisses Ruby on her forehead, and says, "I'm bringing them a peace offering and something to help motivate them.". Ruby asks," What's that?". Roderick replies, "Fish! Bears love fish." Shaking her head Ruby gives him a final piece of advice. "Don't forget the honey.".

Roderick recruits 20 of his finest warriors to track down the Bear colony north of his encampment. Bears can be unpredictable based on how hungry they are. It's why he is accompanied by warriors. Just in case. As he runs through the forest, he can see the owls in the trees tracking his moves. Always observing. Always silent. Always paying close attention. As much as he'd like to snipe them, he knows they are not to be touched. After 5 nights of tracking, Roderick and his pack enter the bear lands unofficially named "The Spider Streams". This is where most of the Great Bears Gather for breeding, eating, fight each other, and to exchange thoughts. Its name was coined after birds flying over, said the multitude of streams flowing together, looked like a huge spiderweb. The Bears tend to be loners but will come together for the survival of their clan. It's one of the reasons why they make great mercenaries. In times of great tribulations, the bears chose a leader and once the conflict is over, they are free to pursue their individual agendas.

Centered in spider streams is a massive bolder. The bears use it to squawk out their thoughts and ideas like some ancient Greek philosopher or actor at an Epidaurus theatre. Roderick will use it to get their attention. He and his pack make their way to the top overlooking a scene of trees and streams. In the distance you can see a snowy mountain range. Roderick takes a deep breath. In unison with his pack, lets out an echoing howl. This causes an alarming disturbance in the bear's colony habitat. It didn't take long before some of the more agitated bears respond.

"What the fuck is this? What is going on? Stop stop stop stop!! YOOUU DOO NOOT BELOONG UP THEERE!", shouts out a bear named Kodi. He is the wartime leader and most outspoken of all the Bears of spider-stream. This was achieved mostly because of his lineage. More of the bears start showing themselves from the tree line. Roderick and his pack make their way off the natural podium and cautiously approach Kodi.

Kodi, unafraid of the wolves, confronts the trespassers. "You are either extremely ballsy or extremely stupid. which is it?", asks Kodi. Roderick replies, "Obviously, I was trying to get someone's attention.". "OBVIOUSLY! And you seemed to have achieved your objective, and then some. You ended up getting all of all of Spider stream's attention.". Slightly clueless as to the gravity of his actions, Roderick tries to explain. "Well, how else was I su...". "HONEY! Where's the honey?", Kodi asks abruptly. Roderick is confused. "Honey?", He asks. Kodi looks around as if to find answers from someone else. "YEA FUCKING HONEY!". I don't know how to make my question clearer.", says Kodi. Remembering what Ruby had told him about the honey, Roderick hesitates with his answer. "I didn't bring honey; however, we did bring fish.". Kodi sarcastically shocked says, "No honey? Let me get this straight. You werewolves traveled this far north for miles to get here from your wolf refuge, right? Then you crawl up on our sacred stone, disrespectfully if you ask me. Then spew out some horrible noise interrupting our peace. You probably want something from us. It's the only reason why anyone ever comes here. AND YOU DIDN'T BRING ANY FUCKING HONEY? Look around you. Do you not see streams full of fish?".

Roderick whispering to himself," I thought she was joking about the honey.". "What did you say? Are trying to be cute with me?", Kodi asks. "I would remind you wolf; you are out of your element. Outnumbered. Outsized. And I am running out of patience. State your business or go home.". Roderick says," We will get you honey. More importantly we respectfully request an audience with your people.". Kodi says, "Well, you might as well take your ass back up to our sacred boulder and bark out whatever it is you're here for.", Kodi commands.

Roderick turns to heads back up on top of the sacred boulder to address the bears. He rehearses in his mind the most effective words to convey how it would be in their best interested to join the cause, then deliver them without further insult. He turns around only to find all the bears are gone. He looks at one of his warriors with a perplexed expression on his face, only to see him shrug his shoulders and say," We should have brought honey.". Roderick gives a defeated look. *"What a waste of time this whole thing was."*, he thought to himself. He begins to round up his loyal companions. Before he heads home, a lone bear, the biggest he's ever seen, walks out of the tree line with honey dripping down his face. "I'm in." he says." I have nothing else going on so let's go collect some fangs. I already knew why you were here". The pace back to the refuge is much slower. The bears inability to keep up slows everyone down. On the third night they stop to rest, set up camp, and settle in for night's rest. In the rush to get back the fact that the bear's given name was never inquired. The curiosity of one of the wolves gets the better of him provoking questions. He asks, What's your name bear?". Overly eager he replies, "Mud.". They all snicker at him. "Mud?", another wolf asks jumping in. Mud looking around wondering what the big deal is repeats himself. "Yea Mud!" Waiting for an explanation, the wolves become impatient. One of them asks, "Well? Are you going to explain how or why you name is Mud, or do we have to ask?". Feeling gitty Mud replies," Nope. I am not going to explain willingly. You must ask.". All the werewolves look at each other in disbelief but want to play along with this bear. Finally, the question is asked, "Why is your name mud?". Joyous Mud replies," It's short for Mudawarr Mudada. It means one who has a round head and provider. When I was born the elders....". "MUD IT IS!", Shouts over one of the wolves with his eyes wide open. "Why are you here? ...MUUUD.", is asked. Mud scratches his belly, somehow knowing one of them would eventually ask the question." He simply answers, "Because no other bear is. I figure. Someone must represent our species. And why not? I need a purpose. I have no life partner, no other REAL reason to exist. SOOO, Here I am.". They all agree that it is as good as a reason as any. With no more questions to ask or answer a restful night begins.

Early next morning, Roderick and his pack resume the journey south to the refuge. On their arrival, they were greeted by Ruby and supporting Generals. Ruby pulls Roderick close to her and presses her forehead against his. She whispers in his ear, "Obeisance my love." He responds with Anjali Mudra, bringing his hands together at his center heart to show his respect and love for her. Roderick sees the curiosity of a newcomer. He introduces the stranger to everyone, "This is Mudawarr Mudada. The only volunteer.". "Mudawarr Mudada?", Ruby confirms, and looks to Roderick. Mud immediately explains, "It means, one who has a round head and provides. Just call me Mud. When I was born the elders....". Ruby quickly turns to Mud cutting him off. "I TOLD him to bring honey. Did he?", asks Ruby. Mud amused replies, "Nope, didn't bring any.". She throws her hands up in disbelief. Ensuring no-one will blame her for this mistake she makes it known to everyone. "Well, I told him not to forget." Roderick, ready to move on asks, "Can we fucking stop with the honey already?". Mud answers, "No, we cannot stop with the "fucking honey". I'd like some if you please." Roderick sends a volunteer out to retrieve honey for Mud. Rudy briefs Roderick on the latest events while he was gone. "While you were gone, I ordered a Company of "Blood Pack" terriers sent off to see if they could track down Dustin, or at least get info as to what happened to him. They killed a crew of hyenas and brought back a wild dog.". He replies, "Show me."

Roderick is led to a muddy pit that they use to keep their captives. The pit is deep with steep muddy walls making it impossible to climb out. Decorating the inside are random bones of unidentifiable remains. Victims are fed just enough to survive for whatever ordeal is planned. Roderick looks down inside to see a muddy, bloody, and tortured creature that used to be a healthy wild dog.

While laughing, this lone wild dog shouts out, "You fuckin cunts! I gladly suffer, hoping to last long enough to see you all skinned and used as cloaks. I will be revered and honored for my hardships. "Unimpressed Roderick asks," What happened to the Greyhound you were tracking?" He defiantly replies, "Dead, following your orders. Unfortunately, we weren't the ones to do it. I Can't say for sure. Likely a dessert for the Komodo. Yea a "doggy treat" We chased him to where those lizards live and was smart enough not to follow him into the sands. If he isn't here, it doesn't take much to figure out the rest." Mud leans over to investigate the pit for the first time. With honey dripping out of his mouth like drool, it draws the attention of the wild dog. "A Bear?" exclaims the wild dog. Mud naively explains himself, "Hi my name is Mud. It's short for Mudawarr Mudada. It means one who has a round head and provides. When I was born the elders...." Viciously the wild dog yells at Mud, "NOBODY GIVES A SHIT BEAR!"

Slightly shocked and embarrassed by the outburst, Mud turns to Roderick and asks, "Rubes, Roddy, are you two done with this dog?" They both nod yes. Mud confirms with everyone else. "Anyone else have business with him?" No-one responds. Inspecting the walls of the pit Mud asks, "Roddy, If I were to just happen to fall in this pit, could you get me out?" Knowing the next move Roderick says, "yes sir". The wild dog interrupts Mud's questioning." I HOPE ALL YOU FUCKING CUNTS..."

Suddenly, Mud jumps into the pit, with jaws wide open and claws fully extended. He lands on top of the dog. In short time he murders the beast mercilessly, displaying ferociousness widely admired and sought after by warlords. He lets out a chilling roar echoing throughout the surrounding refuge. As he turns to look back up at his admiring onlookers, he growls out. "HONEY!" Roderick and his Generals turn to organize their next steps. Roderick calls for a headcount. Bronze," 200 Broncos.";" Baxter; "550 Rams";" Strickland; "400 Eagles; 100 bearded vultures"; "Muscles, 2000 terriers."; Tank, "You have 50 of my rhinos; Ruby, "100 Weres". Roderick nods in approval with the numbers. "And one bear!", Mud interjects. "Just me." Everyone turns and look at him annoyed. Continuing, Roderick asks, "Is everyone fully armored and equipped with their designated weapons?" Ruby reassures him, "Breast plates, cleaves, pauldrons, gorgets, gauntlets, helms. and specialized combs. All custom fitted for each breed for maximum protection and kill effectiveness." Roderick, talking to his Generals, states, "The most important issue is intel. We have shit as far as that goes, and our recon team is MIA. Their last suspected known whereabouts were the sands. We are going to have to deal with these Komodo sooner than expected. It'll be unwise to go into this upcoming fight with nothing. Confronting the Komodo, we'll need a show of force. It'll do nothing to scare off the red stripes komodos, so I expect a fight.". Muscles feeling the need to voice his thoughts says, "Killing one of my terriers instantly gave my brothers and sister motivation to fight, they will be looking for payback." Roderick continues, "We will form a classic battle formation. 40 rhinos centered, 250 rams on either side, 1500 terriers form behind them with 150 broncos form behind the terriers. Depending on how it goes your horses will provide flanking attacks with the terriers. My weres and I will be in the vanguard. The rest of the troops will be in reserve. Ruby, form them how you see fit. The blood pack will remain with you. Strickland, you and your warriors will provide air support. You will Coordinate with Ruby for intel and battle adjustments." Mud feeling left out asks, "And where do I go? what do I do?" Thinking about where to best utilize Mud replies, "You'll be in reserve with Ruby as her personal Praetorian."

Happy about his new position Mud pauses. "I'm a little lost. What's a Praetorian? Is it like, someone that does her makeup and hair to make her pretty?", Finding his inquiry humorous. "No, it's my like my bodyguard.", Ruby replies with annoyance. Mud grins at the thought. "OOOHHH! Bodyguard?", Mud murmurs. Roderick sees that Mud is not understanding his role, so he explains." Yes. If something were to happen to me, Ruby will be the most important person in the clan. I need you, along with the blood pack members to ensure her survival. Mud continues," Soo I'm important then! Ha! I would argue though, that the most important...". Having enough of Mud's nonsense, Roderick briefly loses his patience." MUD! Go see the armorer.". Roderick focuses his attention back to the group. "We leave in 2 days. If any issues arise before then, report it immediately. Once we get to the sands, we'll form into our battle formation. Be prepared for a fight if this goes one way or another. As always, I honor and thank you all for you upcoming sacrifices."

The Werewolf war machine and its allies march east through the mountain ranges onto the borders where the Komodo have settled their community. As they get closer, the battle commanders form their forces into its formation for any confrontation that they may encounter. In the distance they can already see the curiosity of the Komodo have focused their attentions onto their direction. Tensions on both side heighten and adrenaline pumps through everyone's bloodstream knowing violence is inevitable. Ruby and her reserve unit break off from the main fighting force and distanced themselves far enough away as to not be accounted for by their enemy but close enough to effectively respond to changing situations. The vanguard places themselves in the front. Holding their formation, they advance forward. As they get closer to contact, they can see the extent of the Komodo population. Clearly the Komodo outnumber them at least four to one. Their deadly bites and fanaticism make up for their lack of armor and battle tactics. Just like clockwork the red stripes make themselves known by approaching with speed and aggression towards them. A sea of Komodo following close behind with aggression instilled in their minds.

The Lead Komodo meets face to face with Roderick. With intent in his voice he hisses at Roderick, "If you came to invade and claim our lands you fail to bring enough warriors." Roderick meets the lead's tone with his own intentions. "My companions and I have a few questions. Depending on your answers your lands will be the least of your worries. It'll be your lives we secure as our own." The lead laughs in his face. "You're funny. Most say we Komodo have no sense of humor, but you won't be around long enough to find out." Roderick tickled by the verbal bantering asks, "I guess then, I better just tuck my tail in between my legs and go howl at the moon somewhere?". "OOWWWWW! Mocks the lead.". Roderick asks, "A little while back a terrier may have crossed into your lands. He had a message for me. He was being chased by some wild dogs and hyenas. You wouldn't happened to have heard anything about it?" Looking into the distance disrespectfully the lead Komodo thinks. "AAhh! You're Roderick! I do remember a mutt mentioning your name a way back. What, he didn't make back it to you? No, he didn't, did he. That's because we shit him out a long time ago. And as far as your message? Hahaha. Poor wolf pups. If my calculations are correct, your pups are probably being slaughtered like lambs."

Just then the lead throws a piece of paper at Roderick's feet. It reads.
"To kill the tree, destroy the roots."
Terror and rage take over Roderick's heart. The future of his pack is exposed to any attack. Roderick starts barking out orders,

"Strickland! Get word to Ruby to take the reserves and get back to the refuge ASAP. Deploy 250 Birds with her. Our young one's lives are in danger. Muscles, have you ever tasted the blood of a Komodo? Muscles eagerly replies, "Not yet." Roderick says to his loyal friend, "You won't be able to say that tomorrow. Baxter sound the war cry."

Immediately all the werewolves transform into kill mode. Claws and teeth extended. The rhinos nod their head up and down aggressively, as to simulate goring and tossing something into flight. The Rams snorting and kicking up dirt, readying themselves for a charge. Terriers growling, snapping, drool and foam shooting out of their jaws. Broncos bucking, kicking, and shouting an angry bray. The battle begins then ends hours later with the slaughter of thousands of Komodo. The wild killing frenzy and blood lust leaves the Komodo at a critical low. Half of Roderick's forces are lost. Eventually the Komodo scatter and retreat into the desert in which they came. Fortunately for Roderick and his allies, the armor they were equipped with protected them long enough to win the battle. Roderick and his generals take an accurate count of the survivors. The dead will be brought back and sent off to the afterlife properly with full honors. The battle is over, but casualties will not be.

2

VAMPIRE NATION

GOBLES SITS IN A LARGE DINING HALL AND SNACKS ON BLOOD cakes. A dark, dry piece of blood sweetened bread vampires casually snack on to help keep their energy up. He hears laughing and struggling heading toward his direction. The door bursts open and through it, a group of Gobles' foot soldiers drag in their captive. Gobles satisfied with the result of their hunt, grins and shouts out, "Bring me that mutt! Hold him down."

Many find Gobles, at the very least, creepy looking at first glance. But to those with an even more intimidation factor in their personality, would find him frighteningly disturbing. He stands over seven feet tall, pale skin, and is protruding at the joints. He has long sharp fingernails, purposely manicured and sharpened. He takes great joy in slicing then poking his victims to draw blood. It would be a huge miscalculation to view his frame, then conclude that he is frail and weak. He has a reputation to single handedly kill individuals twice his size and weight. Whether the rumors are true or not, many believe the scars displayed on his stomach, which he prides himself on, were the result of a dispute he survived killing a rhino. With shoulder length, silver hair that appears to glow in a full moon, and a mouth full of jagged, pointy teeth; it takes even they hardened warrior to overcome their nerves. Being the head of the vampires, you'll rarely see him wearing any colored clothing other than black. Steal tipped boots, equipped with a heel that can eject mini spikes at will, allows Gobles to weaponize his feet with death stomps and kicks during battle or torture. He especially enjoys slowly pressing these projectiles through a victim's head into the ground and listening to them screams.

Khowl, the designated leader of the hyena clan, repeats the order, "BRING FORTH THE WRETCHED HOUND!". Delighted with themselves, random soldiers join in, "Yes! Bring forth the mutt." A lone terrier is dragged across the hall. Battered and bleeding. Knowl grabs the terrier's mane and pulls his head back so Gobles can get a clear look at him. Knowl says," Sire, the wretched mutt has been brought forth."

Gobles charges forward toward the terrier. The bystanders let the terrier go and scatter away giving Goble a clear path to his victim. He grabs the greyhound by his throat, slams him on his back, and holds him down by his throat. The terrier defiantly stares back making little attempt to resist the strength of this vampire. Gobles inspects the greyhound's features. "Puppy, puppy, puppy. This can be painful... or very painful. Either way, you will die. I already know why you're here, but you can confirm my thoughts. Now, how many of them are you?" Goble receives no response. "You know dog, why do we have to do this the frustrating way? This is how it goes. You tell me the answers to my questions, then I kill you and spoil your plans." Still no answers. Gobles becomes tired of the lack of response. He tightens his hold. Grumbling he asks, "HOW, MANY, ARE, YOU?". Knowing the outcome, the terrier finally speaks. "Come close. I can see that your face is flush!", he replies.

In a fit of rage, Goble finds a mouthful of the dog's neck and bites a chunk halfway through his throat. He continues to drink his blood until his body is limp and lifeless. Goble looks up at the onlookers with angry in his eyes. For a pause it is silent. Then simultaneously they all laugh in euphoria. "That was awesome!", one shouts. Everyone joins in the laughter. Gobles orders, "Find the others! Bring them here, quickly. If they get away, then you will pay." Knowl turns waving off the others telling them, "Let's go losers, you heard him. If they others get away, you will pay.".

Correcting Knowl a subordinate replies," He didn't say we are going to pay. He said you are going to pay.". Knowls pushes him out the door then threatens," No, I'M saying you will pay!".

Talking to himself, Goble blurts out, *"Why are Hyenas are dumber than a pile of shit but they are smarter than a bucket of piss."* Thanani walks in after witnessing everything unfold. She affirms his beliefs," Because they ARE, dumber then shit but smarter than piss.".

As sexy as she is deadly, Thanani, comes from a lineage of black panthers. Her reputation for her seriousness intimidates most that cross her path. She leads the big cats into battle with the ferociousness of the Komodos and killing skills of a Venus flytrap. Once you're in her claws, death is imminent. There's no bargaining with her. You have one option. Die. She puts up with the vampires and follows their lead for her own secret agenda. She has her own ambitions but understands the art of war. She knows timing is everything and brains nine times out of ten, beats strength when strength has no brains. She and her clan have served the vampires loyalty enough to gain their trust. More out of hate for the Weres and love of themselves. The abuse of their cousin grimalkins at the hands of the terriers have left her with no emotions, just revenge and hate. She has unified all the cats except for the Lion clan. Their services are as self-serving as hers. She fights alongside them if they'll follow her lead.

Gobles, pleased to see her says, "The time is near. Our plan is coming together as written. Those stupid terriers have taken the bait, the seed is planted." She informs him," MY plan, has come together. If Dustin takes the route through the sands the Komodos will surely kill him. That should start a conflict within the refuge. That being said. While they are distracted, we will destroy their future seeds. If not, then we with must prepare for an all-out war. And if we do that, we will need to send an envoy to the lions. We can use their help. And it would help to go seek the assistance of the Spider stream bears.".", Gobles says, "Let's not wait. Send word to the bears, and you need to go personally to see the pride. They would see it as a disrespect not to receive our finest warrior.". Thanani agrees. She adds, "I'll send Cajole to the spider streams. If anyone can talk a bear out of its honey, it would be him."

Thanani walks out of the room and summons the Cajole. It is a title more than a name. He is a great persuader, known to build armies on his words alone. He tries to use imaginative words that confuse those listening more than anything. He fights sparingly, finding he can accomplish his desires less painfully if he articulates them with his words, rather the staff he carries with him everywhere. He reports to war room as demanded by Thanani. He walks in proudly with his head up and chest out. Ecstatic to see Thanani as he is for all he greets. Most think it is part of his act and do not reciprocate his enthusiasm.

Cajole attempts to flatter her, "The Great Warrior commander of our illustrious combat forces, the Queen of stratagem and master of tactics. Your beauty rivals your life liquidation. How may I discharge your most onerous injunctions?" She replies, "Your blarney warms my heart, like a pile of shit warms the bottom of a commode. Save your eloquent speech for another prospect. Go to the spider streams. Recruit some of those furry beasts. Offer them what you want and no matter the cost. I don't expect many to join our cause, The bears of spider stream need to be provoked. I'm sure you have some type of locution floating around in your head you can utilize. Cajole giggles and says, "My fancy, the messianic Oration to those four-legged imitation lecturers. I'll gladly implement your will...". "GOODBYE!", Thanani shouts cutting Cajole off. He bows to her and says, "Adieu" Thanani call in Hecate. Hecate is a capable and devoted cheetah human hybrid. Always close behind Thanani, leading the charge, and reenforcing the will of Thanani through his actions. She informs him, "we must journey to pride country. Armor up. The lions are our cousins, but it doesn't hurt to be prepared in case they are looking for confrontation. Also, they may want us to go on a hunt with them to show our loyalty. If that being the case, their prey is more than a handful to deal with. We cannot afford to lose warriors on a hunt we have almost no business being on. If I must explain our losses to the Vampire counsel. They won't understand.". Hecate, looking for more instruction asks, "Will 4 cheetahs and a Bengal be sufficient?". Thanani thinks momentarily to access the strategy. "If the Bengal is Thorn, then yes. If not, make it two.". Hecate nods his head to show he understands, then leave to carry out her orders. Thanani walks into her chamber, looking at a map, and re-imagines her strategies. *We cannot rely on the hyenas and wild dogs alone, even with their vast numbers. My big cats are too few. It is imperative to get at least one pride and the help of the bears. We have enough Vamps, but they are almost useless during the daytime. First thing is first. Lions.*" The sun rises. Thanani starts on her mission to where the lions hunt with four cheetahs and two Bengals. Thorn has little interest in expending energy on lions. He prefers to fight the enemy and doesn't consider them so.

Back in the council Hall, there, plans and schemes are hatched, trials are held, and politicking takes place. Dark and looming, the head of all the major and minor houses are provided accommodations. The hall is centered within the ruins, so all members have easy access, and no member feels superior nor inferior to any other vampire. Goble sits in the highchair, where the head of the vampire nation positions themselves centered and elevated to address the chamber members. Adrina, a mole rat hybrid, scurries in from a large hole in the side of the wall where she has made her living space. Gobles notices and calls to her, "Come here you little rat!". She crawls up his leg and up onto his shoulder. Gobles turns to address the chamber members. "The plans are in motion. These werewolves are a menace. They have not only hunted our food source to almost extinction, but time and time again, they've attacked our stronghold murdering our some of most distinguished ancient house members.". Adrina replies, "They are a menace!". Gobles continues, "They have defiled our civilized inhumanity. These untamed, wild, unreasonable loups-garous and their allies must be eradicated from our existence.". "ERADICATED!", Adrina repeats. Gobles, unphased by Adrina emphasizing his words, resumes. "We will do this! YOU WILL ALL FALL IN LINE AND ASSIST IN ANY WAY I FEEL FIT!". Adrina losing herself in the moment jumps off Gobles' lap and onto his knee. Standing on her hind legs and pointing at the chamber members yells, "Damn right we're going to do this! You will all fall in line! And I'm going to tell you right now that if I see any lack of enthusiasm....". Having enough of Adrina overzealous display of bravado, Goble picks her up, and throws her into a chute meant for unwanted discards.

A Council member asks, "And your plan? We haven't been briefed. We know not what it is entailed? You make decisions without our consent and worse, our knowledge? You are leader by seniority only. You must, by tradition, get the council's approval for any act, that would affect our community. Furthermore, you allow that cat, to command we, and our forces? Lastly, you allow that rat into our chambers to lampoon around in our consecrated conclave. This council..." Gobles lashes out, "I WILL NOT HAVE THIS LAMBASTING!". From a distance Adrina can be heard repeating, "LAMBASTING!". Gobles stands up to speak and intimidate anyone who objects, "If this council refuses to comply to upcoming conflicts. Then I will see it fit to apply heliacal punishment. We are at war! We will be as one!". "As one!" can be heard faintly. To identify anyone who may be averse to him, Gobles says, "Now! Those who oppose these intentions, speak and be accounted for.". No-one speaks.

After 3 days of continuous movement, Cajole makes it to the spider stream, where a bear is in an emotional peroration about his family's contributions to their bear's history and lore. A great house of the Bear clan. Universally recognized by all bear clans to have led them in a great fight against oppression. Cajole sits down to listen next to an unusually large bear with a round face and sticky paws from eating fish and honey. The Speaker goes on about how, as a cub, he followed his father's father to the streams they now settle in. In the distance they can hear "our house has sacrificed...". "Hello friend." Cajole says. The bear replies, "Hello. Would you care for either fish or honey? Both are tasty, and the fish is high in omegas.". Grateful, Cajole declines the offer. "I appreciate your kind gesture sir. But Fish nor honey is part of my staple diet.". Satisfied by the response he says, "More for me." Wanting to endear himself, Cajole begins with his word play. "The fine gentle bear on top of the natural rostrum articulates much to my rapture. Although I fail to recognize emotionally to his sentiment, his locution does move me." Completely ignoring to what was just said to him, the bear introduces himself. "My name is Mudawarr Mudada.". Tickled Cajole replies, "AAHH! Of round face and provider. Your elders have truly observed your features and decided to guide your path with that name. May I compress your name to make it more...high speed and low drag? By all means, I don't want to in any way diminish your parent's legacy. How about mud?" Liking the nickname Mud agrees, "Sure, Ok. Mud it is.". "Tis it is", Cajole says. Grimacing and amazed Mud accepted the nickname Cajole asks, "how would I, a simple fox, adept in oratory, be able to gain the attention of your fellow compadres?". Answering his question Mud replies, "Do you have honey? Because if you don't, then you cannot. Honey is the money and if you have none, then your voice goes unheard." Cajole realizes his mistake and tries to salvage the situation. "I have no honey, but if you'll allow me a moment of you time, maybe I can offer you another type of the sweetest honey, a concordat.". "A whaa?", Mud asks. Let's go to your grotto and talk business."

Thanani and her escorted warriors travel east for what seems to be days to where the lion pride hunts. On the open prairie lands, where they can easily hide in the high grass and hunt their intended prey. The lion prides are vast due to their hunting skills and constant willingness to chase for sport. A typical pride always has one dominate male. The strongest but also laziest. Only ready to kill when necessary. It is the lionesses who are the true hunters. But to gain their service, it is only with the male approval does this occur. Within distant proximity are rogue lions. There are many. Always looking for an opportunity to control their own pride. They run in their own kill pack. Pain in the asses. But virtually unstoppable allies if you can motivate them to fight for you. Thanani makes it to the lands where the lions hunt, and of course there is a commotion. There's a hunt in progress. And the bison are the unfortunate game. They maneuver in massive herds for protection. This does not deter the lions. It encourages them.

Thanani and her crew sit back and watch it all unfold. The lions position themselves in a way to guide the bison into a trap. Five lionesses chase and force the herd into a sharp valley where ten more are in waiting to ambush one unfortunate meal. Thanani waits eagerly on top of a ravine at the end of the valley anticipating the outcome. As planned the herd all charge into the valley in an attempt to escape. And as planned the lions ambushed the bison. Chaos! What the lions did not count on was the bison fighting back. Thanani sees this as an opportunity to not only prove herself to the lions, but to earn herself an I owe you. As the pride find themselves as much as a prey as the ones they are hunting, clearly the head of the bison herd makes his presence felt. Twice the size of all other bison and with twice as aggression. No lioness dare tries and bring him down alone. The leader of the pride, Gur, will not allow this. He attempts to tackle the bison but is clearly having immediate difficulty. Before the lionesses of his pride can act, Thanani rushes in and jumps on the bison back. Two Bengal tigers join in to bring down this massive beast. The other cheetahs provide support. Along with the other lionesses, they prevent any other members of the herd from interfering. Thanani applies the final blow to the bison's throat. She has, in that moment, solidified her place amongst the lions. The feeding frenzy begins. The whole lion pride attacks the dead carcass to appease their appetite for blood. Thanani and her escorts sit back and watch the mayhem unfold. The lionesses growl, snap, and swat at each other for position at the dinner table. Out of breath, Gur calmly heads over next to Thanani, flops down for a quick rest and says, "Look at this shit. Do you see this mess I have to deal with? Everyone thinks I have a great life. They think just because I have a pride of lionesses to breed with. I hang around waiting to eat and play with the cubs all day. They never see these messy scenes play out. They never get to see when I must fight off rogue lions to maintain my pride as the Alpha. Look well and good at my chewed-up, mangled tail. Does this not make you want to vomit?" Thanani sardonically comments, "POOOR GUUUR!". Gur completes his complaining, "I know right? Normally I'd get my fill first then let them eat, but that fucking bison can feed my pride five times over. We can wait. Any of you other big cats want to indulge, feel free to jump into that disaster.".

Almost immediately they all decline the offer. Gur asks, "How's Thorn that big lazy ass fuck? Didn't want to come and see a real cat in action huh? You know he tried to hunt me a while back. That Chucklehead would have gotten me too if it weren't for my twin flame Sheeba.". Sheeba, The Alpha female of the pride hears the conversation and pauses to add her thoughts. "It was an honest mistake.". The feeding continues with Sheeba making her alpha female aggression felt, swiping at her sisters who are taking nibbles of her portion, letting them all know who leads them. Gur tells Thanani, "You know, being here will bring out the jealousy in Sheeba.". Thanani informs him of the bad news, "I have no interest in becoming part of your conquests or pride.". Gur not being outdone says," HA! 1.That's a lie. 2.That's not why she'll be jealous. She sees you as a threat to her leadership amongst the others.". Thanani replies, "1. It's not a lie. 2. I have no interest in leading your lionesses. At least not for this nonsense. We are readying ourselves for a battle with the Lycans. We would appreciate your pride's participation. Acting surprised and insolent, Gur furthers the verbal assault. "HAHA! The Great Thanani and her vampires can't handle a pack of wolves and their raggedy mutts? Your Bengals and Cheetahs aren't up to the task?", pointing to her companions of cheetahs and Bengals. Visibly agitated, Thanani seeks to shut up Gur," First of all, as I remembered it, you and your lionesses couldn't handle one little, itty, bitty, bison without our help. And to attend to your smartass comment about the wolves, they recruited rhinos. Based on what just I witnessed, maybe I should be looking elsewhere for a stronger pride. Thrilled to hear the challenge of rhinos, Gur investigates further. "HAHA HAAAAA! Rhinos you say? Now that's a hunt! Will Thorn be having some fun with us?".

Thorn answers the question for Thanani." Yes, I will be. Where there is one, there are many." The escort team runs over to show their excitement. They rub against him and lie on their backs showing their belly to display submission. He permits them to surround him with low tones of purring while playfully biting at his ears, tail, and legs. This displays their respect and acknowledgement to his dominance. "Well, I'm in! ", Gur exclaims. He gets up to show Thorn his own form of affection by tackling him to the ground and trying to overpower him as brothers do to each other. This friendly show of alpha competition lasts momentarily until Thorn eventually gets the upper hand, to the surprise of Gur's pride. Breathing heavily and walking side by side rubbing against each other, they make their way back to the group of onlookers. Thorn says to Gur, "My old friend. I heard you were doing well for yourself. Now look at you. You did say you'd have the biggest pride anyone has ever seen.". Gur raises and protrudes his chin forward into the air arrogantly. Thanani ends the sickening sight of brotherly love and asks, "Do you want to be the newest member of his pride Thorn, now that you two are done kissing all over each other?". Sheeba butts in, "He's not welcomed to without MY permission, and you aren't either.". Thanani, wanting to deescalate the tension between the two jabs back, "My escorts and I are going to go feed off that beast I just killed so you and your pride can eat. When I get back, we will press reset and you can start off by thanking me first, then I will conduct my business.". Thanani and her escorts leave to eat while the pride, satisfied from feeding, lie down around Gur, Sheeba, and Thorn, to form a protective circle.

Gur trying to calm Sheeba down tells her, "You know you should show her a little bit more courtesy.". Sheeba replies, "I will at some point. After we come to an understanding." Thorn asks, "How are you Sheebs? Been a long time.". Sheeba replies, "Yea! Last time I saw you, you were begging for your life. You tried to make a meal out of my love here. My sisters and I had you on the run.". Embarrassed Thorn replies, "That's not how I remembered it, but ok.". Gur interjects, "That's exactly how it happened!". Sheeba asks, "Why are you all here Thorn? Are you trying to complicate our lives? We are happy here chasing bison around and raising our young ones. Whatever it is that brought you here, is something we aren't interested in. Thorn replies, "My why is different than Thanani's. I'll wait for her to come back and to let the cat out of the bag.". Gur says, "Hahah, save your world-famous puns. She wants us to fight with her and the vamps." "NO! Don't make their fight our demise. We belong here.", Sheeba quickly responds. Gur pleading to Sheeba says, "Come on! It'll be fun. I'm going just because there is going to be rhinos there.". Angrily Sheeba elucidates her convictions, "No, you're going because Thorn is going to be fighting rhinos, and you can't stand hearing about someone else's glory from a distance.". Gur confirms her statement, "Maybe you're right, but I'm still going. And I could just tell you to come with us, but as always, I'll let you decide what you want to do with our family.". "And what about us? Our pride?", Sheeba asks. Reminding Gur, "God damn it! This wasn't part of our plan, remember? We were supposed to have a simple life and raise the next generation of our kind. That's it! Just you and me." Gur responds," Yes, I remember. But for what it's worth, this will help the younger lions practice their skills on some dogs. Sheeba pleading, "It's not that simple and you know it. Our young lions may not live long enough to enact your lessons.". Gur replies, "For me it is." Sheeba realizes there's nothing she can say or do, to change his mind. The glory of the kill trumps her cries to remain home. Defeated and compelled to be at Gur's side, Sheeba finally concedes. Thanani returns and says to the group, "You're welcome for the kill because I know you won't thank me later.". Sheeba wastes no time letting her know their decision to join, "Well, I guess we will be joining your campaign. I refuse to leave Gur without his pride to fight your battles. He'll need his family. The other thing is, I will be included in all the battle tactics. That's nonnegotiable.".

Thanani, pleased with her new allies, reassures Sheeba that her input would be needed in every aspect of the campaign. Thanani further reveals, had her persuasion failed, she would have no alternative but to send in Cajole to recruit them. The thought horrified everyone but was comforted knowing they wouldn't be subjected to such maltreatment.

At the vampire ruin, Adrina tells Goble, "The council members are not happy with your tone toward them. Will you consider maybe eliminating them and their disdain by creating a council more loyal to you and your cause. Gobles replies, "I am well aware of their attitude toward my reign. And I am always considering the possibility of replacing them. I must watch how I execute those ideas. If done carelessly, I could invoke a civil war or worse. Risk being staked myself. Adrina offers a suggestion, "Why not let the Weres kill them off?", That's genius!", says Gobles. Adrina proud of herself says, "Thank you sire.". Gobles brings her off her high and says, "I was being sarcastic. Don't you think if it were that easy, I would have had that done already, a long time ago? Roderick and his pack of mutts have been trying to kill us all for decades.". "Ahh yes sir! You are always right. Then how?", Adrina asks. Gobles thinks to himself, *"How is the question. I have to consider the owls who are always watching and recording my every move.".* Adrina asks, "Why not rid yourselves of those foul arial beasts? They're always looking at me with those hungry eyes and pointy claws. Creeping around, waiting for the right moment to add me to their gumbo of field mice and dungeon rats. I can feel the violence in their soul as they..." "Shut up Adrina! You're breaking my concentration. You know some day I will serve you up to the owls.". Adrina pleads, "No sire, not the owls. I'm sorry. Spare me.". Goble picks up Adrina and throws her into a trash chute. He thinks to himself, *"The rodent does have a point. I first need to distract the owls in some way. Then get rid of the councilmembers. And what about Thanani and those loyal to her? The Hyenas are loyal but dumb as shit. Who can I call on?"*

Just then a messenger makes himself known announcing the return of Cajole. "Cajole has returned from the spider streams sire. And the scouts report Thanani is a day away with Gur and his pride." Excited Goble replies, "Excellent! Your task is complete. Send in Cajole and go away!". Cajole walks in feeling accomplished. "Salutation Grand Mikado of our terraform. The Imposing Oligarch of our commonwealth. The..." Gobles stops him before the verbal parade of ass kissing begins "You must want to go down the awesome and majestic chute of shame with that naked mole rat.", pointing toward the side of the wall. Adrina repeats, "Chute of shame!". Gobles asks, "tell me of the news from spider stream. And speak so I can understand.". Cajole briefs him" I was able to recruit 100 bears to our cause. It will cost enough honey to satisfy a thousand Elephants!". Goble expecting the cost," As is expected. What else?" "WHAT ELSE?", Adrina adds. Cajole continues, "After victory, they require the lands of the wolves to settle. I was ordered to agree to whatever terms they required. That was what they really wanted.". Angrily Goble lashes out, "WHAT? I did not expect to just hand over the wolf's refuge!". Cajole reasoning with Gobles says, "Sire, you don't have to give them the lands after we win. Just make them think that they'll get it.". Gobles coming to his senses says, "Correct! I will need your oratory for a special mission. Go seek the assistance of the raccoons. I will need them in the coming battle. And be quick about it. The wolf moon is almost upon us. The werewolves will be at their most dangerous. Get as many as you can.". Cajole responds," Very well sire."

The following night Goble stands on the balcony of a ruin while looking down onto what was once a thriving society. He sees Thanani walking along side Sheeba leading a band of big cats. Followed by four cheetahs, two Bengal tigers, the main pride of lions comprised of 15 other lionesses and an equal number of younger members of the pride. Gur and Thorn providing rear protection. Gobles smiles at his latest achievements. Acquiring the forces of Gur and his pride solidifies his army as a formidable fighting force. Seeing a pride of lions heading a charge in the coming battle will surely inspire others in a way that can never be calculated.

Gur eagerly approaches the band of warriors and says, "Welcome Gur! What a wonderful, how would Cajole put it? Spectacle. Adrina will tend to your pride's needs. We will have a briefing in the council chambers." Gur corrects Gobles' "My pride is more than just your spectacle. My pride is a well-trained elite fighting force." Gobles replies, "as you say." Adrina perched on Gobles shoulders chimes in, "as you say.". Sheeba confronts Gobles, "There is an issue needing to be addressed. I hear the Vampire council is not supporting you. Or am I mistaken?". Taken back by her knowledge of the situation, Goble pauses and stares at her before answering her, "They will fall in line, or pay the dearest of costs. My Vampire nation will do its part." Sheeba exposing Gobles' weaknesses asks, "And your hyenas? Wild dogs? Are they loyal enough once they know we lions will be involved?". Gobles, feeling uncomfortable and disturbed with such bluntness replies, "They are. We shall discuss all details in full whilst in the council chamber.".

Cajole reaches the scavenger lands the racoons tend to gather. He finds a quite area in a wooded area. He sits down and opens an article from a Widener Law Symposium journal he found on the journey northwest of the vampire ruins. Re-inventing the Past by Sherri J. Braunstein. As he begins to read, an adolescent attempt to find out what the fox is doing without being noticed. Cajole, without looking, starts to acknowledge his visitor, "Do you know why abandoned shipwrecks are both romantic and adventurous squirt?". Surprised he was discovered he replies, "No. And I don't know what a shipwreck is." Cajole educates him, "Because the forgotten stories they tell are interesting, sad, and mysterious. They also may contain awesome treasures and artifacts that could teach us about the past.". "You sound funny." Squirt says. Cajole agrees and continues, "I know. It's on purpose. I like using funny words to confuse people. I amuse myself. I think it's fun looking at the express on people when they try to understand what I'm trying to communicate.". Squirt asks, "Why?". Thinking, Cajole tries to dumb down his thoughts. He says'" Well' I'm always reading so… well. I really don't why. It's just fun to me. That's it.". Squirt says, "You're weird. I'm leaving now. Nice to meet you shipwreck.". Before Squirt can leave Cajole asks him, "Can you tell one of your elder's Cajole is here and would like to talk to them funny?". Squirt says, "Sure.".

Back in the chamber, Gobles informs every one of the situations. "As we speak, Roderick and his forces march east to confront the komodos. Thanani what's are force count."

She replies with, "Sheeba, Gur, and the pride equal 30 fighting members. We have thirty cheetahs and Thorn has gathered forty Bengals. There are a thousand wild dogs and 500 hyenas. Cajole recruited one hundred bears.". Gobles adds to the count. Thanani continues, "Cajole is recruiting raccoons.". Adrina laughs and says, "Raccoons.". "RACCOOOONS?", Knowl asks. Sheeba responds, "Yes Raccoons! They are the sworn enemy to the eagles. They will prove valuable if we can recruit them." Goble chimes in, "We will. I have 50 vampire warriors also.". "Is that all?", Thanani asks. Goble sarcastically answers, "We have Cajole. Maybe he can kill them by boring the enemy to death with his lecturing.". Everyone laughs in agreement. When everyone quiets down Thanani continues. "So far our forces number around seventeen hundred fighters without the addition of the racoons. It'll be hard to say if it's enough. They Could have an upwards of 3500. Or nothing after a battle with the Komodo. Problem 1. They have rhinos. 2. Roderick and Ruby are master tacticians with trained skilled warrior clans fighting with them. Alone without allies, they are just as good as we are, if not better than us. Together as a force? True war machine. A head on battle is unwise. We must move quietly and swiftly. I propose during the night. Obviously, we all are more effective that way. We kill their younglings and attack their rear guard. IF, we get the raccoons, it will be important that they engage their birds. The birds are their early eyes and ears. The other issue are the Rhinos.". Gur says," Leave the rhinos to me.". Thanani tells him," once you figure it out let us know. Besides that, overall, we have the size, strength, and speed. They do have the numbers and discipline warriors.". Pleased with the initial plan Gobles expresses himself, "You have come up with a solid plan Thanani.". Sheeba corrects him, "WE came up with this plan. As in. Thanani and I.". Cajole returns with good news, "Add Bandit and 300 raccoons to your count. Easy as pie.". "Cajole!" Adrina exclaims. Before she can get too excited, Gobles picks her up and tosses her into the chute. Thanani updates her count, "Two thousand total.". Cajole, proud of himself begins to let everyone know how he recruited the racoons," I told them their kind is like shipwrecks. Forgotten, abandoned, but valuable and needing of recognition for its past glories. I also told them. The Eagles were saying how they were a bunch of overgrown, thieving rats. The later worked.". Gobles says, "Excellent. It is time to put intent into action.". Thanani completes the meeting, "We will begin our war march in two nights. The wolf moon quickly approaches.".

3

THE SUFFERING

Grand Owl Boris-

DURING "THE SUFFERING" EACH ANIMAL HAS ITS OWN SPECIFIC
rite of passage designed to train their species in combat. That is
only the first part. Animal clans naturally form into alliances.
Thus, their training reflects that. As the animals progressed
through the second phase, their specific talents complement each
other on the battlefield. For instance, the rhinos and rams work
together in a charge. This battering formation is only matched by
the elephant's charge. With Weres riding their backs, as well as,
on the backs of a flanking Bronco calvary engulfment, you can
see how this applied could fruit success.

Only male Rams are sent to their suffering. For they are the
gender that grows battle horns. Their female counterpart mainly
breeds, help raise the young, and keep their males focused on
battle. As the young grown old, they are taught and mentally
programmed to fight. Ares, the god of war, is the only deity
they worship. All others are insignificant. From the moment
they can comprehend, it is instilled into their souls. Once the
ram's horns grow visible, they are marched off to the notoriously
treacherous high mountains just before winter. Thrown into the
brutal elements at such a young age seems unimaginable to other
species. It is demanded by their god. To prepare for war, it is the
upmost of importance to suffer the elements first and foremost.
Harden your mind, body, and soul. Strip your very being of any

self-awareness and individuality. It is the warrior next to you that is more important than you. That is the ram way. That is the only way. As the male Rams train and the weak weeded to the rear. The strongest of them hold the most prized position in a battle formation. In the front and middle of every formation. That is until they are paired with the rhinos. Once they get older and train with them, the closer to rhinos the better. It is why the rams war cry is "FRONT AND CENTERED!". A war cry they take seriously. Before the cold and blizzards to come, the young are set up in their training area which is basically rocky land high in the mountain with embedded caves for the older ram trainers. The first order of business consists of ascending and descending all mountain ranges. From the peak to the base and everything in between. Being able to traverse through brutal weather conditions will be the building block. Once they're march begins nothing can stop it. They must finish or be left behind to fend for themselves. Very few are able to complete this trial on their own. The march continues over 1000 miles throughout winter until the following spring into an open flat summit. That is where the second phase of their training begins. The rams are taught battle formations and tactics. They are taught basic fighting skills and weaponry. The young rams are taught their history, the art of war, camaraderie, duty, code of honor, and above all else, self-sacrifice. As their skills become honed and sharpened, they are pair against each other. Both as a team and as individuals. As the stronger and more aggressive separate themselves from the lesser. They are segregated to what they call the "Big Horn" brigade for specialized training such as reconnaissance, black ops, and scout assassin's platoon. Once the rams are proficient in all aspects of battle training, they are sent to the final phase of instruction. ICC or Interspecies combat conditioning. There they learn how their skills and abilities will be applied to a war machine. They will practice tactical skills and prove themselves worthy to fight as a unit.

The Bronco's suffering is quite different. From the youngest of age, the Broncos of the Great Plains are taught self-awareness and self-respect. They admire speed, grace, and technics in battle. Some may say their vanity is cherished more than war fighting, but this is mostly misunderstood. They just think if a horse is going into battle to fight and kill, they might as well look good doing it. Others think the Broncos are generally overly vain and prefer to die in battle then to survive with scars and imperfections. Their war cry supports this misconception. "The Beauty of Battle!". From the moment they can trot each foal is fitted with a helm that has a single lance protruding from the forehead. This acts not only as armor but also a weapon. These young horses are rarely seen without them being worn. This allows them to look like a unicorn. Something that they take great pride in. Once they have reached their maturity, they are given a harness and saddle with steel wings spreading out as if about to fly. These wings are sharpened, rivaling any sword. The result is an intently visualized Pegasus. A beautiful but frightening sight to the enemy. When these charging Broncos perform a flanking maneuver, even the Rhinos take pause with the idea of an oncoming collision. The ancient Spartans would love the "Beautiful Death" they bring with them. While completing the suffering the Broncos young, run hundreds of miles a day, and as they grow older and stronger, weight is added to their caravan. Speed, stamina, and strength are their focus in training. The fastest and strongest of them are sent to become part of an elite unit proudly named, "Perseus' Own". Every Foal strives to be a member. The second phase of every Broncos suffering consists of perfecting their skills, grooming themselves, and bragging about how great they look doing it. After perfecting their skills and primping, they are sent to the final phase of their training, Interspecies Combat Conditioning.

Of all the sufferings, the Rhinos training may be the most physically brutal, but also the least complicated. No tactics, no trickery, just brute strength, and power. They endure excessive beatings to toughen their skin. It is wrong to believe that the skin of a Rhino is just a tough hide. Their skin is thick but sensitive. They spend a vast amount of time scaring themselves to build up a callus over their body and prevent battle punctures. For this reason, the Rhinos inherently are envious of the Broncos. The two groups equally respect each other but could not be more opposite. While the Broncos systematically dispatch their foes, the Rhinos prefer to crash, smash, and leave a bloody mess everywhere. During the Rhino's suffering, the young bulls and cows push, pull, lift, smash, charge, eat, and rest. Just to do it all over again, but harder and faster. Unlike the other species the Rhinos do not go to a "special force" for specialize training. There isn't much use for a hulking brute in a unit where silence and secrecy are first and foremost. Instead, the Rhinos, who are the strongest, are honored and utilized to set the example for others. They take great care in ensuring their horns are as long and lethal as possible. As a final initiation before sent off to the main fighting force. Each Rhino is branded with a lightning bolt on the front upper leg. An indication of completing their rite of passage. After what they call "The Burn", they are allowed to profess their war cry, "GORE, GORE, GORE!".

The Lycon's and Terrier's suffering together. These two species have always been close. Knowing that the terriers have evolved from the ancient wolves, the terriers almost feel as if they are wolves themselves. Just more civilized. The Weres and Terriers complete their challenges together. As one. But the Weres tend to be less disciplined and focused, hotter headed and likely to redline. Thus, they must go through a specific ordeal to help them suppress their urges. Once the pups stop suckling and are able to hunt independently, they are sent to a city ruin closest to the refuge to begin training hunting feral cats they call "Grimalkins" or "Grims". The bigger cats were highly offended by this practice and became instant their sworn enemy once it was discovered. Both the weres and terrier species must show proficiency in catching, then killing the felines, until they can move onto bigger prey. Those who fail or refuse, become themselves victim to the pack. As they become bigger and stronger, they move onto prey up to 5 times their size and weight. Mostly male are sent to this training to become warriors. The exception is when the female gender cannot conceive healthy pups. Failure to produce a strong litter will give them an alternate opportunity to contribute. If achieved, it is highly honored and revered. A female warrior terrier is looked up to by all. The strongest warriors can earn a position in the "Blood Pack."

The Eagle's suffering

The Eagles, as well as those strong enough to fly with them, have the longest and most complex suffering out of them all. They are expected to accomplish more than the others and thus, making them an invaluable part of the war machine. Their death is felt extraordinarily different than any other clans. Their nesting homes and nurseries are protected by the strongest and most brave of the species. Their training and upbringing are considered most important. It is the foundation of their very being, and in turn, must be guarded before anything else. Once the eggs are hatched, the hatchling is welcomed into the world with a ritual some may deem insane. They are carried as high as their protector can carry them in their claws and dropped. Before the impact of the ground, they are caught. This ritual is repeated frequently until the Eagle hatchling is able to fly on its own. For the protector to miscalculate, or inadvertently failing to retrieve the hatchling resulting in its death, will in turn be the cause of his or her own demise. Birds of prey that come of age and can fly on their own, are sent to their suffering in all climates and terrain. They are taught how to survive, first as a group, then as an individual. They are taught how to kill, care for themselves, recon, observe, and signal. Their final test before integrating with other species will be that of strength, speed, and endurance. It requires them to fly long distances, carrying heavy cargo, extreme diving, and accomplish it as quickly t as possible. Only when those designated responsible for their training are satisfied, will the trainees move on. "Death from above!" Their enemies will come to remember their war cry.

4

ON THE MOVE

IN THE COUNCIL HALL THANANI LAYS OUT HER BATTLE PLANS TO Goble and the Vampire council, Thorn, Gur, Sheeba, Kodi, Adrina, Bandit, Cajole and Knowl listen in. "The battle we are going to undertake will take all our efforts. We will need to execute with speed, intensity, and with finality. Most of Roderick's fighting forces will be engaging with the Komodo resulting in an unknown outcome. We must anticipate that not only will he prevail, which is likely, but also that he wins handily with minimal casualties. With his forces preoccupied, that leaves the future of all their vulnerable. Eliminating their future fighting forces will initiate the beginning of the end to this never-ending war. This will be the foundation of our ultimate victory. It'll be a coordinated attack on the younglings on all fronts of their first phase training. I expect the first phase of our objective to be completed easily. Once this is accomplished, we will gather outside the joint interspecies training grounds to attack their younglings in their 2nd phase of training. Make no mistake, DO NOT ALLOW THEIR AGE AND INEXPERIENCE TO FOOL YOU. The 2nd phase younglings can fight effectively. I anticipate more casualties then less. The key to our success is overwhelming numbers in force. The violence of action is to our advantage. Leave no survivors. Show no mercy. Upon completing phase 2 of our attack, we will undergo a campaign to overtake and build a solid defense of the Lycon's refuge. We will await Roderick's returning forces and eliminate him and his allies once and for all. Bandit, your raccoons will be attacking all Eagle nests, along with the birds that train with them. Gur, Thorn, and Kodi will take the Bengals and bears to attack the Rhinos. Knowl, take the hyenas and wild dogs for the Weres and terriers. Sheeba and I will take the big cats to eliminate the Rams. Goble, you will evenly distribute your forces to each group. Your mission will be to seek and kill any creature looking to escape. This is especially important to those assigned to the raccoons. Send your best with them. It would be a mistake to let someone escape and have them get word back to Roderick. Cajole, take any necessary precautions and preparations you will need. Travel east. Your only function is to recruit willing warriors to rally for our cause and quickly return with significant forces. Any questions?". Adrina asks," What are my orders?". Thanani sarcastically replies," Stay here. Protect the Council Hall while we're gone, and make sure no-one gets out of line.". Adrina, not catching on to the ridicule, nods her head, accepts the orders and says," What! Yes, I can handle that!". Everyone turns and stares at her. Goble says, "Well, I am pleased. The plan you and Sheeba envisioned sounds solid. I see success. If there are no other concerns, we leave tomorrow night. Ready your people."

Ruby is moving her forces back to the Lycan's refuge as quickly as possible without stretching her units too far apart. She has a sinking feeling in her soul that the most precious of their future has already met their gods. They must stay together. If they are to engage the Vamp nation army, they will be most effective as a unit. Her other worry is that of her twin flame Roderick. How does he fare fighting the Komodo? She is certain they will be victorious, but at what cost? She can't think about that right now. The younglings, their future, protecting their future is all that matters right now. She yells out each clan's war cry. "LOYALTY OVER LIFE! GORE, GORE, GORE! FRONT AND CENTERED! THE BEAUTY IN BATTLE! DEATH FROM ABOVE!". She vocally displays her love and loyalty to them, giving them extra energy, confidence in her leadership, and reinforcing pride in themselves. They return her intensity by pushing harder and faster. Roderick and his allies are battle-weary. The fight with the Komodo has taking its toll, and only time will tell if there will be more casualties. Fighting with Komodo have a delayed effect on the true casualty count. A Komodo's diseased bite can take days to cast its death finality. Body armor is effective in this respect. Roderick's pace is far slower than Ruby's for obvious reasons. Roderick is about a day behind. He musters up his commanders for a report. Roderick calls for a head count. Muscles replies," Six hundred terriers, eighty stallions, one hundred rams, 40 rhinos, one hundred and fifty eagles, and 20 vultures.". Roderick contemplates the numbers in his head and thinks to himself," *Sixty wolves. That's Approximately one thousand and fifty.*". Roderick gives his final instructions before heading out back east. "Keep an eye on those injured and expect some to die on the march home. Death from fighting Komodo have a delayed effect. Muscles and Bronze, you two lead the march back for those who are ready and able to fight. Strickland and his birds will maintain over watch and air superiority, keeping the lines of communications open and active. They will relay any messages of changing event. Send your fastest ahead to Ruby for support and reconnaissance. Brick, Baxter, and I, along with a handful of our strongest warriors, will be following behind with the injured and meet you as fast as practical. If there's no questions, let's move out.". Muscles, Bronze, and Strickland depart with approximately 740 warriors rush to help Ruby: While Brick, Baxter, and Roderick escort 310 injured soldiers slowly behind.

Thanani and her forces begin the massacre that would come to be known as, "The night the roots died". That night would dictate the rage of coming ages. It ended as quickly as it began, with no warning, leading to no resistance and no survivors. The innocent, along with those that protected them, had no chance. The Vampire nation and its forces gather miles outside the interspecies training camp.

Thanani says," I assume no casualties, so no need to take an account for numbers. This assault will be quite different. We must assume that the recruits here will be well trained. I expect a clear victory with some casualties. Make no mistake. It is essential that we end this as quickly as possible. Our intel suggests that Ruby is on her way here, and we must be ready to fight a brutal battle. Gobles interrupts," I don't see these younglings, even trained as they are, to be much of a resistance.". Gur annoyed replies," Then you're stupid!". Tensions start to rise. Leftover aggression from the taste of blood earlier. Gobles stands up and asks, "What did you say?". Gur stands up with Sheeba rising to her feet behind him. Her sisters backing them both up as the they growl and stare at Gobles. Gur repeats himself," Then. You. are. Stupid!". Gobles' personal guards stand to defend their leader. Gobles closes the distance between them and says," Not as stupid as your insolent words.". Knowl adds," Oh! What do we have here?" Unwisely getting up. Thorn warns him, "Knowl, whatever your intentions are, it would not go well for you to act on them.", while poking him on the chest. Kodi starts to laugh. Thanani attempts to refocus the group, "GENTLEMEN! And Sheeba, ladies. We must focus on what is ahead of us. We cannot allow our emotions to distract us, or we will all perish. As soon as our presence is detected they will sound the alarm and our mission will become increasingly difficult. It is of the upmost importance that we attack with precision, aggression, and intent. The Bengals and Lions will attack from the north, more as a diversion. The Vamps and bears will attack from the south. With the vast numbers, the Hyenas, wild dog, and raccoons have, they will secure the east and west the perimeters, picking off any beast looking to escape. It is important to cut them off from the refuge. ", Gobles complains, "I don't see why we just don't form a line, and attack with a head on direct assault. You overrate these younglings. My vamps and I could easily...". Frustrated Thanani explains," Because they are trained to be most effective that way. We must break their ranks by causing confusion. We must not underestimate these young warriors. With all due respect. This is most effective way." Knowl remarks, "Whatever." Gur having enough of the insults finally snaps. He grabs Knowl by the neck and shouts, "Why don't you shut your fucking mouth!". Sheeba grabs him before the situation gets out of hand. She grips his wrist and calmy whispers to him, "Sweetheart, I understand. Not now.". No-one acts on the outburst, and they continue without further incidents. Thanani issues her final orders," We begin in 30 minutes. Gur, Sheeba, Thorn. Take your cats and begin your stalking. Get their attention enough to draw them out. Once we have drawn them out, Kodi and Goble will attack. Knowl and Bandit, hold your positions. Send in your forces in a double envelopment if they begin to scatter and retreat. Kill them all. Any Questions? Sheeba asks," What's plan B if plan A doesn't work?" Gur answers her, "Attack.". Thanani agrees," Yes Attack. Kill anything that moves."

Adrina is back in the council hall consulting with the head of the council. She attempts to impose her authority over them. "While the master is away all inquiries, questions, concerns, and or situations shall pass through me. I alone will make a final decision and I will ensure that..." Offended the Head of the council members grabs Adrina and erupts," Shut your mouth rat! You have no authority, nor say in any matters of this chamber. You are nothing more than a midnight snack. A distasteful one at that rate.". Adrina squirms away and escapes the grip. She dives into the trash chute and yells to them, "Gobles will know of this insult.".

Head member speaks to the chamber members, "Gobles has shown great distain for this chamber, He has not followed proper protocol, He has taken half our forces and allowed that cat to dictate to us. US! THE GREAT VAMPIRE NATION! WE? Dictate to WE, the highest and evolved of species. We cannot stand for this. It is we who should be leading and giving orders in this fight. The Vampire Nation has never, and never will be, subjugated to Weres, Bears, Dog, or cats. I call on this chamber to come together in unison to outlaw this rogue leader and declare him an enemy of the nation. As well As those who may follow him and that panther. What Say You?". They all respond with," AYE!". Head member continues, "It is done. Gobles and those who may follow his horde, are here by declared an enemy of the state. We will send an emissary to his forces demanding he lay down his arms, return, and stand in this sacred chamber for judgement. And if anyone finds that rat. Feel free to snack.". Adrina scurries off after listening to the treason.

Traveling far east to gather more willing forces, Cajole sits high looking over a wide open plain. He witnesses a curious event. Hard to see clearly from here. Troop movement heading west. Observing and wondering who they could be. What is their purpose? Cajole thinking to himself, *"Now what do we have here? Prospects perhaps? Too far away to determine the make-up of this army but they do look formidable from here. Not clear of hostile intent but surely doesn't seem to be a civil group. Wait could that be a....?* "Just then Cajole feels a sharp deep pain thrusted into the back of his neck. It happened too quickly to respond. He feels his body being lifted off the ground. Had this creature wanted him dead it would have been done. The death grip around his neck, and the fear that overtakes his body causes him to freeze up and not make a sound or even move. He feels and sees his limp body flying hundreds of feet off the ground moving at a high rate of speed toward the marching army. He's being carried by some sort of raptor. As he draws closer, Cajole knows what he is experiencing is only the beginning of something far worse than he could ever imagine. An army much bigger than he's ever imagined.

Meanwhile, back at the training grounds outside the refuge. The Big cats, led by Sheeba, move into position. Sheeba orders the cheetahs to position themselves on either side on the far flank because of their speed. This tactic will hopefully contain the younglings from out flanking them, then funneling them into the center where they can be contained in its killing field.

The lionesses will be on either end of the center front line for reinforcement, and the biggest and strongest cat will be centered. Exactly where Gur and Thorn wish to be. Knowl, Bandit and their divide their forces in two, then begin their march into position. Not taking seriously the task ahead of them.

Knowl complains to Bandit, "This is a joke. We shouldn't need these intricate battle plan tactics to defeat these younglings. If it were I in charge I would say; Bandit, go round up your striped rats and go have at it? Call me in the morning. Seriously. If you and your coons are just supposed to run around causing a diversion attacking targets of opportunity. How dangerous could this be?". Bandit replies, "Ha-ha Yea, I bet the worst of my species can overtake this so-called training ground. We could just get into position and just rest out this battle. I mean, why burn all this energy when the others are going to be doing all the hard work?". Knowl agreeing," Yaa See? I need someone like you around to keep everything into perspective. I'll have a few of my forces run around acting like we're doing our part.". Bandit replies," YES! The dumbest and weakest of the group.". Thanani and the big cats sound the start of the operation with a roar that echoes for miles. The Big cats begin their stalking making as much noise as possible. Without a pause, their battle cries are met with sounds of alarm. Weaponized, armored younglings react. As expected, they form a strong front line. The traditional formation as taught with the Rhinos centered and Broncos flanking. The few Weres and Terriers hold rear-guard with the young rams in the event of an attack from behind; it being clearly the weakest part of this formation. Before the younglings engage in battle the rear-guard forces bark out orders. "CANTABRIAN CIRCLE!" All younglings repeat this order. "CANTABRIAN CIRCLE! "Several leaders shouting out to their warriors. "WE HAVE CONTACT ON ALL SIDES!" As rehearsed the younglings form a massive circle with the strongest of the rhinos and rams forming a hard outer shell. The stallions place themselves just inside the circle with the Weres, Terriers, and Birds of prey riding all their backs to repel any attack from any angle. Gur looks at Thorn, Gobles looks at Kodi, and Sheeba looks at Thanani. "ATTACK!"

All the Big cats charge the circle with the cheetahs leading the assaults. As they get closer to contact, the eagles take to flight and circle around behind. The Vamps mount the Bears from the south as they charge. All involved show their fangs anticipating a massive collision. Leaping into the air, the first wave of cats engages and is met equally by Terriers and Weres. The Bears smash into the smaller sized well armored rhinos and rams. The younglings are outnumbered 5 to 1 but to their credit, stand their ground. Soon the sheer number of Vamp nation warriors begin to overtake the skilled younglings. Sheeba shouts to Gur," Where the fuck is Knowl and his forces?". Gur screams," We are taking unnecessary casualties.". Thorn offers his thoughts," I'm going to throat that bastard! Thanani orders Kodi to send someone and find out what is going on with Knowl. Kodi orders his trusted commander Sherrian to investigate. He tells her," Go get Knowl and have his forces engage. She acknowledges the order," Say no more.". Sherrian is a tested Kodiak Bear. Know famously for fighting off and killing 3 blood pack wolves to protect her cubs. Tragically lost the cubs once the fighting had been done. She has a personal vendetta against all Weres as a result. Shortly after her search, she finds Knowl, and his forces settled in the refuge camp. Sherrian questions Knowl, "What the fuck do you think you're doing? We are engaging the enemy! You are ordered to engage the enemy." Knowl amused, challenges her, "By whom? Because I don't take orders from you or Kodi? Not even by Thanani for that matter. I only answer to Gobles." Sherrian, "And answer you will." Claws extended, Sherrian reaches and attempts to apprehend Knowl to drag him back. Before she can grab hold, she is attacked by a dozen hyenas and wild dogs. They snap and grab at her forcing her to back away while inadvertently falling into the refuge's muddy pit. Unable to escape, all the hyenas and wild dog surround the pit laughing at her. Knowl mocking Sherrian, "Hehe, looks dirty down there. Yuck. Sit there and relax awhile. We real warriors will go finish this. Let's go boys! time to kill."

Back at the training camp 2/3 of the youngling meet their gods as the battle rages on. As a pause reaches the ongoing melee, the hyenas finally arrive. Bloody and battered, Gobles, Thorn, Gur, Sheeba, Thanani, and Kodi turn to see a well rest Knowl and his forces. Gobles points to the younglings and says, "Well? WHAT THE FUCK ARE YOU WAITING FOR?" Knowl snaps out of his twilight, looks back to his followers who are waiting for instructions, and barks, "ATTAAACK!". Charging at the younglings, they come to a complete halt. Realizing what is heading toward them. Ruby and her reserve unit smash directly into the side of their attacking force. They surround the younglings forming a protective barrier against the aggressors. She yells at the paused onlookers, "If it is death and blood you desire? Well, with us you'll find it at the end of my sword!". She holds up a sword to display the blood stains left over on the blade from her first contact.

Gobles starts to panic, "We must retreat and finish this another day. We cannot win this battle!". Thanani replies, "No! Here and now. We have the advantage! They are not at full strength. They are fatigued from their march. Sheeba agrees," She's right. We must not waste this opportunity." Gur asks," And where is Roderick? His forces are nowhere to be seen. Maybe he didn't survive his return.". Thanani pleads, "The longer we wait, the faster we lose our advantage.". Sheeba suggests, "Send in those fucking Hyenas Gobles. It is their fault this isn't finished yet.". Knowl attempts to defend himself," This not my fault! I did exactly wha…". Gobles interrupts, "Quiet! You will take your forces and finishes this. NOW!". Knowl is hesitant and replies, "How am I supposed to engage this circle phalanx?". Thanani corrects him and says, "It's a Cantabrian circle, and by attacking it.". Sheeba yells, "Yes, figure it out."

Knowl gathers his forces and briefs them on the plan of attack. Knowl huddles up and says, "Ok listen. We'll go in waves. First wave will be more of a distraction while the second wave tries to penetrate the inner circle and break their phalanx from within…?? I guess. I don't know I've never planned battle strategies before. If this doesn't work, then I'll figure something else out."

As Knowl moves out to execute his plan the rest of the forces sit back to watch the pending disaster unfold. They all take bets on Knowl's success finding the pending nonsense soon to be displayed.

Sheeba says, "Look at this idiot. What are the chances he succeeds?". Thanani says 25%.". Gur having less confidence says, "Not even I say 15%. What'll you say Thorn?". Thorn replies, "10%.". Not to be outdone Kodi inputs, "5". Jokingly Gobles blurts out, "I say 85%!".

They all look at Gobles with a silent pause, and in unison let out a roaring laugh. They wait eagerly to see who is right.

5

A New Threat

CAJOLE IS DROPPED TO THE FEET OF AN ANIMAL WITH BLACK hairy feet. His Vision slightly blurred by an unexpected flight. Cajole and this being are surrounded by others who have similar feet. Furry black legs are all he can make out for now. He hears heckles. He hears a voice, "Smash him into the ground!". Another laughs and says, "Hehe, Yea smash him!". Random voices shouting, "No eat him, no wait. Smash him, and then eat him!". The apparent leader shouts, "LOCK IT UP!" and immediately there is silence. On lookers walk away knowing the spectacle has ended. Four armed personal guards stay for protection grabbing Cajole and picking him up. He begins to examine him. Sniffing and Poking. Then sneezing in Cajoles face. He drops him and says, "You are a teeny, little runt. I could smash and eat you. But that would clearly leave my belly unsatisfied. I would have to find about 20 more of you for it to be worth my time. You have a stink on you that makes me lose my appetite anyway.". Cajole recognizes his species and says, "You're a silverback gorilla! What an example of perfection to your kind! Although I've never seen a silverback in person, I have been told of their grandeur. My name is Cajole. By species I am a Vulpes Vulpes or Red Fox. I do have homosapien DNA as well, but not nearly as much as you I would imagine. I mean look at the specimen before me!". He replies, "Your flattery is somewhat annoying. If this, is you every day, then I bet wherever you came from, you wear out your welcome long before you arrive?". Cajole says, "My council and diplomatic skills are well renowned. I am a valued asset to the Vampire Nation and to those who choose to utilize my abilities.". The mysterious figure is amused, "VAMPIRE NATION! Hahaha. I am not impressed with this Vampire Nation. I have heard about their squabbling with the Werewolves and their allies. They even have the big cats doing their dirty work because they are too weak to do it on their own. This endless war between them will come to an end. But at my hand. I will bow all their heads. I will crush them all if they refuse my command. My scouts are all out now, reporting to me the actions of their troops. For all I know. Thanani and Ruby are about to destroy each other in what looks to be a bloody battle. Roderick and his band of broken and lame are apparently useless currently. This may be far easier than expected. Either way I have 10,000 able bodied warriors ready and eager for blood.". Taken back by how much he knows, Cajole says, "This is disturbing. May I suggest a proposition? I ask that you allow me to act as your mediator. I would be able to convey your thoughts and demands to both conflicting factions. There by, achieving your goals without bloodshed. Your army grows stronger. No Lives are lost. We all live peacefully thereafter." The unnamed figure wants clarification and demands, "Plain language rat!". Cajole tries to make his thought as simple as possible, "Provide me transportation to the battlefield and I will convince them to surrender themselves to you. We all live happily ever after.". "For what?", in response, "So you can reveal all the intel of my war party to them? As if it would matter. I have war elephants, beasts of burden, gazelles, hippos, rhinos, the largest of the primates, Andean Condors, rogue lions HAHAH! Whether you act at the pleasure of my will or not, my conquest is a juggernaut. It is undeniable. Irresistible. Why not let the two small fighting factions kill each other off and go clean up the mess? Clearly you can see this would be a better alternative, no?". Cajole see the logic and replies, "Indeed. Your scouts have accurately reported the situation between the VN and Roderick's forces. I would assume that they also reported the value of their great fighting skills and training regimen. This could be of great value to you. Imagine how they could increase the effectiveness of your army with their battle tactics and skills. You could take on armies three times your size.". Slightly offended he replies, "As if there was one! But you do have a point rat.". Cajole attempts to correct him, "I'm a fox.", Angrily the figure picks up Cajole by the scruff. He looks Cajole in his eyes close to his face and says, "You are a rat! A Red fuzzy tailed Rat! Mealy-mouthed, starting to aggravate me, useless rat!" Not wanting to escalate any further, Cajole lowers is tone and replies, "As you say, a rat. And what do I call you, your most merciful excellency?". "You can call me Frank.", he says. Cajole pauses. Frank reacts to Cajole saying, "What did you expect? Some long, drawn out, five-part name with titles and achievements?". Cajole remains silent. Frank thinks of a title to satisfy Cajole's confusion. "Ok, how about, Frank the Silverback? Not bad. But not good either I assume. To you however, it is sir.". Cajole accepts and replies, "Frank the Silverback it is sir. How may I be of assistance to you?". The two walks through Frank's encampment. Frank shows Cajole all the intricacies of his military camp. Temporary training grounds, rest areas, weapons, and armor. He shows him all the manpower he has available at his beckoning. Especially the war elephants. As he gets to the end of his tour, Cajole see death, rotting bodies, chewed up skeletons, decapitated heads, and random body parts. He witnesses the entrails of unidentified creatures until they get to their destination. A large enclosure filled with half dead animals of all kinds. Cajole looks in absolute horror hoping that it's not his fate. Frank asks, "Do you see? A deserving ending to those who oppose, betray, or reject me. This could be you. This could be your VN rulers or Roderick's refuge. It makes no difference to me. I have you witness this not to inject fear, but to stand witness to my greatness and power. I can be gracious and rewarding, but also ruthless and murderous. You will go. You will tell them what you see here. You will convey to them a stern warning. They choose their fate. Do you understand? Is there any part of this, or what I've said, that would suggest that I am not serious?". Cajole terrified at what he just witnessed answers, "No sir, without question sir.". Frank gives his last order to Cajole, "Go. Go tell them all that you have seen here. Let them know what choices there are.". Cajole asks him why. Frank replies, "Why? You know that is an interesting interrogative. I don't have a tragic story to tell of revenge, or a royal lineage to fall back on. Not a narrative of destiny or chosen by the gods. No Ideas of weeding out the weak. No. I just enjoy killing. I love seeing the spirit fly out of a lifeless body. The joy I feel having so much power in the palm of these hand. Ha! Yes, I do it because it energizes me, it arouses the primitive essence of what we really are. Savages. Animals. Even the lowest of life kills something for some reason. Love, self-survival, or to possess things. Surely my reasons to kill for pleasure is just as good a reason as any. Look at you. Don't you kill something for your reasons? I figure why not rule why pleasing myself. I don't expect a rat like you to understand. You go tell your VN rulers. Prepare themselves.".

Frank signals to one of his personal guards. Cajole is immediately grabbed and carried off to the nestling area of the raptors. The guard dumps Cajole at the feet of a condor. Twice as large as any eagle he's ever seen. If Cajole didn't know any better, he would have it thought to be a thunderbird. The mystic bird of South America. This raptor could easily remove his head from his neck within seconds. The Guard relayed the message that his orders are to take Cajole back to the refuge battlegrounds and return. The Andean condor nods his head that he understands. He takes to flight circling Cajole. Diving toward him, the condor snatches Cajole off the ground and takes to flight. Personal Guard asks Frank," Sir, was that smart showing that fox our encampment details?". Frank replies, "No, it wasn't. It was genius. I showed that rat exactly what I wanted him to see and believe.".

59

As Cajole is being carried over the military camp he sees what Frank has told shown him is not only true but Cajole can see the vastness of his war titan. Cajole starts to understand that there is a serious threat heading toward everything he knows. All has now changed. He begins to think of ways he'll be able to convince the VN about what is heading their way. Even more, how will he be able to get Roderick and his forces to understand this threat? Or would it be best to save himself and warn his species? Cajole knows what it's like to live in harmony with the VN. He has experienced Roderick, the refuge, the spider streams, lion pride. He knows how to survive using his cunning and wit. Frank, however, is the unknown. From what Cajole can see, only death and misery await. Do the owls know of this? And why wouldn't they say anything. Wouldn't a threat like this be the exception of the rule to their code? Cajole knows they are to remain neutral in all matters, but does Frank understand this? Does Frank even care? Each question asked solicits two more questions. He hopes to himself that the flight will be quicker rather than longer. As they get closer to the VN ruins, Cajole asks the Condor to land for a quick respite. They land by a quiet stream with tree cover and open an open grassy area. Cajole walks over to the stream to sip water. As he sits to gather his thoughts and next moves, he hears rustling close by. It's a familiar smell. A smell that hasn't hit his nose in quite a while. Normally, another time and place, that smell meant food. Not in this instance. "I know it's you Adrina. Quit hiding. I know your scent." says Cajole. Happy to see him, Adrina sprints out of hole in the ground and yells, "CAJOLE! Cajole, Cajole, Cajole, Cajole! What a relief to see you! We're in trouble, we must go! The council! The council! Treason! They...". Cajole holds up his hand to Adrina's mouth to quiet him and says, "Stop! Catch your breath. Slow down.". After a short pause and Adrina calms herself to breath she says, "Cajole, we must warn Gobles. The Vampire Council has voted to apprehend Gobles and detain him for an examination. Even worse, there's a bounty on me! The Council has ordered any vampire who finds me, can eat me!". Cajole devastated says, "This is not good. Much worse than I can ever imagine.". Adrina replies, "Yes, it is. Can you Imagine? Me? A snack for some vile vampire?". Cajole says "I can't, but that's not what I'm referring to. There is an army heading our way. This army is bigger than anything I've seen. Many times, bigger then both the VN and Roderick's forces combined. And their leader is a psychopath. I'm not sure if he prefers to rule or kill.". Adrina worried she'll be left behind pleas, "This is a huge problem. Take me with you. I can't stay here and well... I need protection, to be quite Frank.". Confused at her choice of words for a split second, "Cajole notes, "That's the name of the psycho I was referring to. Never mind, come on, let's go get my transportation.". They quicky shuffle their way over to the waiting condor. "Holy Shit!" Adrina exclaims, "That is the biggest bird I've ever seen!" Cajole replies, "Yes. And I couldn't tell you if he's the biggest of his kind. For all I know he could be the runt of the nest.", nervously giggling at the thought.

The three takes to flight. They can see the VN ruin headquarters from above. As they pass by, they can faintly see activities and movement going on. Wondering what is happening, Cajole thinks to himself how unusual that is. Must be connected to the uprising and coup pertaining to Gobles. During the flight, Cajole explains everything that has occurred to Adrina. The Elephants, cages, and Frank himself. Adrina does the same. Mostly complaining about how she was treated by the council, and what she plans to do if ever given the chance. It wasn't too long before they had landed again for another break. As they mingle about, Cajole sees an owl doing what they are born to do. Observe and report. Nothing else. Sitting slightly camouflaged by the tree branches he says nothing. It is forbidden for the owls to get involved in any matter. They refuse to take side and always remain neutral at all times. Cajole calls out to him, "You are a Great horned owl are not?". "I am." Responds the stranger.

Cajole, curious asks, "How do I address you? Do you have a name?". "Quickly the owl replies, "I am Quaid. And you are Cajole. Your companion is Adrina. But I apologize. I am unfamiliar with the enormous creature that has appeared to have captured you. Do I dare to say that he is, an opposing figure? Much larger than any I've ever seen.". Cajole says, "By the tone of your words, it's confirmed that you have no idea of what is transpiring. I feel a little better knowing that you and your owls have not turned a blind eye, knowing what I know. Adrina, try your best to buy me time with that condor to explain to the owl here what we know. Maybe the great owls can be of assistance.". Cajole spent the little time he has left, going over all the details. He convinces Quaid to talk to the Master Owl for further actions. The three of them takes to flight again, understanding that time is of the essence. Every moment that passes, lives are lost, and Frank grows stronger. The feud between the VN and Roderick's forces seem petty compared to possible onslaught on its way.

6

THE HYENA CALAMITY

As THE HYENAS ATTEMPT TO BREECH THE DEFENSES OF RUBY'S
forces, two emissaries arrive with an armed escort of skilled
vampire warriors. They approach with a rolled, wax sealed letter
from the Vampire council in their hand. Emissary, while looking at
Thanani and handing the proclamation to Gobles, says," I see this
battle has not been executed as cleanly as you expected.". In jest
Thanani replies, "Not yet, we'll allow Knowl to embarrass himself
for a little and we'll be back on track shortly.". Emissary catching
on to the sarcasm snickers and replies, "Unlikely.". Gobles shouts
out in an outburst, "WHAT IS THIS?". The Emissary snatches
the paper out of Gobles hands disrespectfully and begins to read.

*"By order of the Ancient and Most Sublime Vampire
Council. You are hereby ordered to cease and desist
all aggressions, violence, and actions toward any
forces. Furthermore, you are ordered to surrender
all your combat arms and submit yourself, as
well as all vampires under your command, to our
conveyers. Whereby you will be detained for an
examination, to be determined if your actions
warrant a trial for the crimes of conspiracy, treason,
and other unlawful acts deemed criminal against
the Vampire Nation."*

Signed Executor of the Vampire Council

The Emissary crumbles up the paper and shoves it in Gobles front pocket and says, "Seize the accused! If he resists your apprehension, you are authorized to stake him at your discretion.". Gobles responds," THIS IS OUTRAGEOUS! HOW DARE YOU SHOW IMPUDENCE! I DEMAND THAT YOU...". Emissary reaches into his jacket and asks, "Are you resisting being secured? Because you demand nothing.". Gobles freezes in place knowing he is in a losing situation. He warns the emissary, "My memory lasts centuries. I will remember this moment in time. And we will revisit your disrespectful actions.". Emissary replies with a confident tone, "Maybe we will. But I have a feeling that likely we won't. Take him away.".

The vampire forces are removed from the battlefield. Thanani and her Generals helplessly look onto the arresting caravan exiting the theater of operation. She looks back to Knowl's calamity failing, then back to awaiting ears on the next steps.

As Knowl's battle plans fail with huge casualties, he calls back his forces to regroup. Without hesitation he starts complaining and making excuses. "You fuckers are useless! Why can't we penetrate this damned formation?" A random warrior replies, "Sir, we try to leap over their formation and get the business end of the spears on the inner circle. Those Rhinos and Rams can't be moved from their position." Annoyed at the remarks Knowl says, "I can see that dumbass! We must commit to this attack. I need... What the fuck is going on?". Knowl notices in the distance Goble and the vampire forces being escorted away. He orders a retreat and back to a safety of Thanani and her army. Thanani call for a headcount. Gur, "My crew is good, 20. The cheetahs lost 4, their total count is 26 able bodies.". Thorn reports Bengals lost 3 total 37 and Kodi reports 93 bears ready to fight only losing 7. Bragging Bandit reports, "300 coons ready to go again. We didn't suffer one casualty.". Knowl returns and begins his tirade,". What the hell is going on?" Thanani reluctantly replies, "Gobles has been seized by the council for examination. What's your headcount? You look like you lost half your forces.". Knowl disregards what was asked of him and says, "Now this is a disaster! I can't believe the council would actually...". Thanani grabs Knowl gaining his attention and interrupting his panic, "What's your head count?". He replies, "Well, I don't know. I haven't even gotten an opportunity to...". Thanani interrupts him again demanding," Go take a head count so we can come up with an effective plan to finish this. The wolf moon is tomorrow night, and we still don't know the status of Roderick's forces.". Knowl questions, "You expect to keep fighting without Goble and his vampires?". Thanani replies, "I expect you to do what I told you to do!". "Yea right or what?", challenging her. All the Generals stand up and fall in behind Thanani grabbing the handles of their weapons. Their actions set the tone sending a stern message to Knowl and his kind. Knowl receives the threat and nervously says, "Relax! Calm down! No need to raise the hairs in the back of your neck.". Knowl goes to reorganize his troops. Shortly after he returns, and reports 1332 soldiers left. Sheeba remarks, "1809 warriors. What do their numbers look like?". Gur takes a quick glance and guesstimates, "800-900?" Thorn gains their attention and points to a disconcerting arrival, "Look! About 700 more.". Thanani, feeling the violence of action to her advantage has been lost, thinks to herself, *"1500 to 1600 for them now, we have 1809."*. From a distance and closing in fast. The first group of backups arrive and join Ruby and her warriors. Kodi Lashes out at Knowl, "This is your fault! Had you attacked with the rest of us, we could have slaughtered each group as they arrived. Now they are all together as one force!". Knowl defends himself, "Me? My fault? Why you are a hibernating, honey eating, pile of crap! Don't blame me! If you...". Before another word is said Sheeba attacks Knowl at his throat with blinding speed. Knowl desperately kicks gasping for air, clawing at her trying to free himself and get away, but without success. Sheeba's sisters and the teenagers of the pride surround her to protect her from protesting Hyenas. Knowl slowly dies, his lifeless carcass is tossed back at the onlooking wild dogs as if a warning to the rest. With the blood of her prey dripping from her mouth, Sheeba shouts, "Now, to the rest of you, fall in line and do your part or be subjected to the same outcome! Pick your new leader and have him or her report to Thanani as soon as possible.". As Thanani and her Generals regroup to come up with a plan. Ruby and her leaders regroup and begin to organize their next steps.

While traveling to the ongoing battle, Cajole notices a caravan that appears to be identified as part of a VN transport convoy. The markings are clearly declared on the banners. It's the VN Examination Guardsman. No ordinary Vampires or foot soldier would be assigned to it. The best warriors the VN have to offer. They must be. The type of missions they take on require them to be the strongest and most elite skilled amongst them. Cajole and Adrina agree they must be somehow involved in the return of Gobles. They ask their transporter to land in front of the speeding convoy. The convoy comes to a complete and sudden holt before crashing onto the three.

The Emissary calls the convoy to a halt. He recognizes the obstacles in his path and says," Cajole, Adrina. And whoever or whatever that creature bird is. Curious meeting you here. Removed yourselves from our path. We have been tasked to apprehend and return Gobles to the council members for examination. Adrina whispers into Cajole's ear, "I told you. It's all true.". Having a little fun the emissary says to Adrina, "AAAHHH! I was told I could have you as a snack if I find you. But alas, I'm not hungry, and I have to carry on. So, if you could be so kind as to remove yourself from our path, we'll be on our way. Or we could remove you all forcefully?" Cajole replies, "Force is not necessary, may we speak with Gobles?". "NO!", the emissary snaps back. "And this is your last warning!". The emissary draws out sword from his scabbard. They all move out of the way to allow the caravan to pass uncontested. Cajole gives them a warning, "Frank is coming. He brings with him death." Adrina adds, "And I'm not a snack!". The emissary ignores the warning and thinks to himself, *"Hm? Whatever that means."*. They take to flight heading to the refuge killing field. As they ascend to a higher altitude, a deafening scream cries out from the condor carrying them. Almost immediately the bird starts descending into a nosedive, spinning, and erratically falling rapidly. The raptor tries its best to regain control of his flight but to no avail. Adrina starts screaming," This is it! We're all going to die!". Through the disorientation, Cajole sees that the landing won't be as bad as it would seem. Into a muddy water muck, they all land. After regaining their senses, Adrina starts thanking all the gods he knows of. Then curses all the gods of death. They can, from ground zero of their crash landing, see that the vampires have deployed a large metallic arrow through the bird designed to kill mostly anything that it's aimed at. Cajole immediately realizes that this current event, will delay the message he has for both fighting factions. Cajole says, "we must move quickly. Clean up and gather yourself together. We must keep moving. You have five minutes. Adrina replies, "Those Vamps. I'll remember this.". Cajole says, "I'm sure you will. When you're ready, I'll carry you so we can move quicker."

They continue their campaign across the lands, which in and of itself is an adventure. Along the way they fight, hide, and talk their way out of danger. Avoiding much larger prey that would have them as lunch or evening snack. Through streams, rivers, fields, and wooded areas, they only stop for a short breath and water. Cajole begins to think of his family and how this situation will impact his skulk back home in the fox burrows. A land where all foxes hunt, breed, and live out their simple lives. Fatigue starts to set in. They must rest before they become too weak to keep going or fight off any predators. They find what appears to be an abandoned den. After a few hours rest they continue their journey without any further issues.

Ruby grateful to see reinforcements arrive, embraces Muscles, Strickland, and Bronze. She greets them saying, "It's welcoming sight to see you all here with your crew. Noticing a lot of dead hyenas and wild dogs littered throughout Muscles mumbles, "Undisciplined mutts.". Bronze follows up, "What's your status?". Ruby replies, "As you see. We need to get back to the refuge and regroup, but at the same time, must stay put and wait for Roderick. We can't allow Thanani to get in between him and us. I think if our wall holds strong, we'll be ok. How far is Roderick behind you?". Strickland reports, "About a day or so march. Hard to be accurate, he has the injured with him.". Ruby says, "Perfect, just in time for the wolf moon. I know the rest of you could care less, but something about that moon magnifies our strength 10-fold. It attracts wolf packs from everywhere to gather and kill. Thanks to Strickland's birds we're able to fly in any supplies we need for now. Once those Big cats and Bears decide to engage us, it should be of a huge concern to us all. Strickland, send word to Roderick of our status.".

Thanani goes over a new strategy with the others, "We must break their formation. The Bears and Big cats will be vital in this perspective. We will have to concentrate our forces in on specific area. Kodi, your Bears will lead the assault with the big cat in coordination with Bandit. We'll need the raccoons to get behind the lines and create havoc. It is crucial to create panic and pick them off separately. Roderick's forces aren't back yet, and I got word that they're a about day 's march away. They have about 300 crippled and wounded. We'll send about 200 fighting warriors as a diversion. If they take the bait, we'll attack the responding forces. If they do not, then those forces will form a blockade and engage the returning wounded, or if need be, maneuver back as the situation changes and the battle unfolds.". Kodi notices Mudawarr is with them. Realizing no-one knows who Mudawarr is he says, "One of the Bears from Spider stream. He's probably the biggest bear you'll ever see. Formidable, but silly as they come. At least that's his reputation. I don't know him personally because he tends to stay to himself, but bears are changeable. I'm sure he can be persuaded for the right price. I imagine if I were to imply certain misdirection, he could create the unexpected chaos you're looking for.". Pleased with this opportunity Thanani replies, "Perfect! I'll declare a parlay. I will leave it up to you to communicate something clever to Mudawarr. As we negotiate, we'll deploy our distraction. Thorn, you will take the best 20 bears, 5 cheetahs, 10 Bengals, 30 raccoons, 35 Hyenas, and 100 wild dogs with you and head east toward Roderick. Ensure you are noticed as you depart.".

Thanani signals a parlay and Ruby excepts. The leaders of both sides meet in neutral ground then begin to size each other up. Centered and opposite each other, Ruby faces Thanani. To Ruby's right, Bronze faces Sheeba and Mud faces Kodi. To Ruby's left, Muscles faces Gur and Strickland faces Bandit. The blood pack positions themselves behind Ruby. Mirroring them behind Thanani are the lions of Gur's pride.

Thanani breaks the silence, "So here we are. The irresistible force and the immovable object. This was unavoidable. The slaughter and crimes against our kind committed for your training purposes and or pleasure. The killing of the Vampire Nation's young? Those acts of violence that your kind, and your allies have committed, needed an equal reaction. Clearly you understand this, and it would be in your best interest to lay down your arms and subjugate yourselves to our rule. You and your warriors will be treated with all the honor and respect due. There is no disgrace in surrendering."

Ruby replies," HAHA! That's what all apprehensive commanders say when they don't really want to earn their victories. As far as any 'crime' committed? I could list just as many as you. Maybe more. You align yourself with the Vampire Nation? A history of murder and deceit. I wouldn't be surprised if they're plotting your demise right now. I see Gobles is not amongst you. He was observed being escorted away. I wondered. Was this all a ruse or set up? Can you say for sure that the Nation hasn't handed you over to our forces disguised as a 'battle assault'? Either way we will not lay down our arms. And we will not subjugate ourselves. We will, however, fight until the end. If it's meant for us to perish, here and now. Then our conscience will be pure, clean, and ready to be judged by our gods.". Thanani agrees," It is true I'll give you that. The Vampire Nation is a distasteful and unappealing entity to deal with. And yes, they are murderous cunts that need to be eradicated sooner rather than later. But that would be a different time and place. For here and now though. It would be in yours, as well as our best interest, to comply with our demands. There is no escape. The youngest of all your kinds have perished, the younglings at your Interspecies training are at a critical low. I sent a kill squad to finish off what's left of the injured and wounded, to include your better half. Even without the Vampire Nation, the chances of this ending in your favor are little to none.". Ruby confirms the possibility, "That maybe so. But if this is our fate. If this is what the gods have intended for us. Then yours is the same. This battle, this war? Will be the same for you as it is for us. Everyone here may survive. The Vampire Nation may thrive on, murderously. But you. YOU, Thanani will not. You will answer to your gods at the same moment that I will answer to mine." Kodi looking at Mud, begins his deception, "Ruby, did you know you had a disloyal amongst you? Did you realize that maybe, at least one member among you, is not who he appears to be?". Ruby pauses and replies, "What is that you're babbling on about?". Kodi says, "Well, I'm not saying that you may have a bear name Mudawarr here fighting on your side providing intel to us. I'm just saying you may have someone. I mean, how else would we know Roderick is a day away, with a platoon of injured warriors from your battle with the Komodo? How else would we know about the younglings left behind? Again, I'm not saying it's Mudawarr here, but I'm not saying he isn't either. I'm just saying.". Rudy starts to lose her bearing, "Shut your mouth Bear, before you end up with boiled honey poured down throat.". Mud chimes in, "It's a bad way to go.". Kodi senses he is effecting the his opposition continues, "Tell them Mudawarr. Tell them how you gave us the ins and outs of their operation. Tell them how you helped us game plan their ultimate downfall.". Just then Mud leaps at Kodi attempting to take his throat. Strickland lunges at Bandit but misses. Bandit scrambles away screaming, "PARLAY, PARLAY, PARLAY!", and hides behind Gur. All parties involved snap into a fighting stance, readying themselves to strike their opposites. Behind each negotiating commanders you can see and hear the war groups preparing themselves to charge at a moment's order. Grunting and growling. Drawing out their weapons. The Blood pack scramble to grab Mud and pull him back from Kodi. The Lion pride do the same with Kodi. Cooler heads prevail although tensions and adrenaline still run high. Rudy finishes the parlay, "There will be no surrender or any deal. We will see you on the killing fields. Thanani concedes to her decision, "So be it.".

Each side separates and regroups back to their respective sides. Thanani compliments Kodi on a job well done. He giggles while wiping some blood off of his face from being mauled by mud. Ruby's camp launches into disarray. Ruby barks out orders, "Grab him! Hold him down!". Two Rhinos grab and slam Mud to the ground. Ruby jumps on chest and jams a blade under his throat. Claws extend, drool seeping between her teeth dripping into Mud's eyes. She demands to know, "WHAT THE FUCK WAS THAT? Are you a spy? Did you betray us? Are you a fuckin mole?". Mud truly terrified for one of the few times in his life and baffled replies, "Mud No! Absolutely not! I have been true to this cause. Whatever this cause is! I'm sorry I don't know. I don't know what they were talking about!". Pressing the matter further, Ruby threatens to end Mud's life by digging her blade deeper into his throat. "YOU LIE!", she growls, "I should gut you right now!". Mud dares her, "Then do it and be done with it! I have done everything that has been asked of me. I never have, nor ever will betray the cause until my contract is through.". Ruby thinks for a moment to gather her thoughts. She raises her blade from the kill strike realizing this is what they want. *"This is how they defeat us. Divide, mind games, cause mistrust."* She backs away from Mud and orders the rhinos to let him go. She extends her hand in apology and assistance to stand. "I'm sorry Mud. Tensions are high and I allowed my emotions to get the better of me.". He replies, "No problem. I will serve as best I can. You have my word. It's all I have at this point.". Ruby turns to those witnessing the scene and makes a decree, "If I fall this coming battle. And it is because of the betrayal of this bear from the Spider streams, Muduwarr Mudada. You all have a sacred duty to end his life in return. Those are my death orders. So be it.". Mud finalizes her edict by sealing it with his own words, "So be it. I would not expect any less.". Ruby gathers her troops, "My chosen few. Nothing else matters. Not before, or after this moment. We have no choice but to fight. We have no choice but to kill. Look within yourselves for strength. Your strength is your comrade's strength. Look to the warriors beside you who sheds their blood. Their cause is the same as yours. We are one unit. One family. It does not matter the starting point for each of us. Yes, we all are uniquely beautiful. We have one purpose, one mission, one focus. We have one enemy. Use your rage, your anger, your wrath. Let our enemies feel your emotions through violence. The outcome of this fight is unknown. But I can tell you this. If we fight as a family, we will win this battle.".

Opposite Thanani prepares her comrades through words, "Now that the mind games and sizing up are over, let's turn to action. We're going to stick to our attack plan. Kodi, you and your bears line up in a phalanx. Gur and Sheeba, disperse the big cats evenly on each side. We'll have the raccoons formed closely behind. The hyenas and wild dogs will be formed up behind the wall. Once we commit to contact, the coons will attempt to overwhelm the front lines trying to get through the smaller spaces under the wall causing disorder behind the lines. Hopefully we can force them to break their wall and pick them off separately. Keep one cheetah at the ready to message for our 200 reserves. They should be able to attack from behind in support to finish this fight if need be. We barely outnumber them, but they are an extremely well discipled fighting force. We all have our reasons for being here. Channel that reason when you feel like exiting this battle. Know that if you are to be breathless for eternity, you live on through your fellow warriors. You will not be forgotten nor lost in the abyss of time.".

Both sides ready themselves in the ways that they need to. Some pray to their gods. Others quietly look to the skies and surroundings one last time, hoping it isn't their last. Gur and Sheeba lie playfully with the rest of their pride. The Tigers go to a local water hole to get a final bath. The Bears eat honey and roll in the grass. The cheetahs sleep and rest while they can. Thanani practices her killing skills and thinks of alternative plans of action. Meanwhile in Ruby's camp everyone is on high alert. They rotate shifts standing guard. Ruby takes a moment to herself and looks into the night sky to speak to her life partner knowing he'll never receive the message, *"If after this fight I fall, and we never see each other again. Know that I will be looking over you. I will be following you. Always protecting you in the afterlife. And if it is meant to be that we be apart. Do not walk alone. Find a better companion for yourself then I ever was. Know that you have my blessing and support. I will be waiting for you and those accompanying you with opened arms and a loving heart. Now I have business to attend to. I hope that I have made you proud.".*

Ruby stands up, grabs her armor and weapons, then places herself on the front lines with the rhinos. With the blood pack closely surrounding her providing protection. Birds of prey landing on the rhinos backs to either side of her. Bronze approaches, with finely shined armored walking up behind the rhinos. They separate to make room. He kneels down lowering himself to offer Ruby an easy climb on top of him. She hops up and puts on her helmet. Facing Thanani and the pending battle. Muscles joins them. Mud makes his way through the crowd to stand next to her. Finishing the last of his honey he looks at her. She looks to him and says, "Loyalty over life". He looks around to his fellow comrades then to spider stream bears on the opposite field of battle, "LOYALTY OVER LIFE!"

7

THE OTHER SIDE

Master Owl Boris-

THE CATS, AS A GENERAL RULE, TEND TO BE TWO SIDED IN MOSTLY everything. One day they fight with each other over hunting, family raising, breeding, and killing. The next day, when the time arises, the cat's loyalty and unity rivals that of the Terriers. Up until the Lions are 4 years old, they spent most of their days play fighting with each other, sparring for position in the pride, learning hunting skills from the lionesses of pact. They watch as the older members of the pride take to hunting and killing. Once the lion young become strong enough, they are expected to participate in a group hunt. Meant to build unity, a family bond amongst them, they are sent out to kill for the pride. Failure in this respect is seen as a major disgrace. Not just for the hunting party itself, but also the pride. The lioness will almost always be a member of the pride, expected to produce the next generation of lions. The males however, their future is less then stable in the pride. They are tolerated and welcomed to stay if the Alpha male allows them to stay. The main mission of the males is to protect the females and cubs from other threats. But this is a delicate balance. The moment the Alpha feels that he has a rival, that young male is removed from the pride one way or another. This male most likely will form a coalition of rogue males. An extremely dangerous group. Their only desire is to kill and form their own prides. The other cats are much different. Bengals, cheetahs, panthers, and all the way down to the smallest of their kind. These cats aren't nearly as organized and close to each other as the lions are. Though the lions fight better as a team, the other cats are much better stalkers then the lions. The cheetahs use their speed, Bengals their strength and ferocity, and panthers their patience. They all have quality hunting skills designed for killing. There are few times in history these cats come together for a common cause. When this happens, the force created is virtually unstoppable.

Hyenas and wild dogs are nasty beasties in their own right. As different as these two species are, they tend to get along with each other as much as they fight. The two species all fight in gangs, never engaging in a fight alone unless they know they can win. Always trying to outnumber their enemy. Strength in numbers is their fighting philosophy. Most hyenas and wild dogs are happy go lucky. Making fun of life and situations. Can't seem to go through a moment without a sarcastic remark. Never taking themselves or anything else too seriously. Unless of course their lives are threatened. Because of their miscreant attitude, their military tactics, bearing, discipline, and skills are almost nonexistent. The lack of seriousness when called for annoys all other species. Others do find comics relief in their failures whether they are intended or not. Long ago the two species joined forces to fight against the lions causing an extreme loss of life on all sides. Eventually all sides saw the uselessness of the killing and formed a truce. But knowing they would always need an alliance with each other for protection, the two species became closer, like the Weres and Terriers relationship. There is only one leader voted in by the clan. Only when he or she dies or is unable to lead, another is voted in. The voting process and title is a matter of formality, these species ultimately get their orders from the Vampire Nation. They feel it's easier to allow others and make the hard decisions for them. They serve the VN for their own sense of purpose. Another reason they are dislike by other species.

The Great Bears of Spiders stream were once a proud and strong community clan. At one time, an organized fighting force dedicated to each other and their community. That was a time before the Spider stream settlement. Before their laziness and isolationism. The Great Bear clan fought decades of oppression, where they were hunted down and killed by Packs of Weres. At the time Bears weren't unified, organized, or mobilized. They kept to themselves in small groups. Easy to attack by large packs of Wolves. Until one Bear, who viciously lost his family decided, this cannot continue. He built a sense of bear pride and self-worth in all Bear communities. He led an expedition of bear warriors, systematically eliminating all threats. He led a coalition of bears to undertake the acquisition of Spider stream that was once infested and controlled by the werewolves and those they tolerated. They turned it into a thriving Bear sanctuary. A place only bears felt comfortable going to. After a long age of peace, most bears became scholars and educators. Others longed for the fight of glory past. They sold their combat services to the highest bidder. Very few bears nowadays fight for long gone honor. Remembering what bears can do, other species refrain from attempting to engaging in warfare with them but would rather hire them to fight for their causes. The Bears live be a plutocracy system. Where the wealthiest and most prestigious family rule what they consider a lower class of Bear.

The Foxes are a curious species. They are very secluded and hardly ever mingle with other species. And when they do you have to be always on your toes. Foxes always have an alternative agenda. Rarely will they show their true intents and are thought of as generally untrustworthy. Their true motives disguised, as well, as their true loyalties. The only thing you can really rely on, is that they will come to the aid of their own kind. To gain the services of a fox for your cause is a great accomplishment. Their services are just as, if not more important, then some of the great warriors in other species communities. For their sizes these Foxes, when provoked, can inflict serious injury on any aggressor. Looking for any fox is like looking for a needle in a haystack. They are more likely to find you first. When they're services are sought out, it is usually for reconnaissance or emissary purposes. They spend all their lives practicing their evading and persuasive skills. Every fox hybrid has a say in their community. Everyone gets a vote. Everyone takes part in decisions concerning their community. Once the majority has made its intentions known. All honor the outcome with zero resistance or push back. When called to vote, everyone is expected to participate and make their choice known.

Out of all the species, the racoons are the most miscreant. Always up to no good and always looking to cause hate and discontent. It doesn't take much to convince a raccoon to fight for you. They don't need to be reasoned with or even bribed. A fair cause or reward is justified enough. Their true joy comes after seeing the calamity from the results of their actions. In this regard, they work well with the Hyenas and wild dogs. If any armed group wanted their enemy camp to experience a chaotic scene, clearly the raccoons would be more than happy to do the job. Their mischievous nature is prized and deployed mainly to inexperienced war camps. Even a well train veteran unit find it difficult to show discipline and bearing in the mist of one of the raccoon's operations. No one really knows who leads them or knows how their culture hierarchy really works. It appears to outsiders, that if the raccoons are causing mayhem, they're happy.

The Most complex of them all is the Vampire Nation. The Vampires see themselves as a civilized, orderly superior society. They hate being dictated to, even by their own. But they do have a code they follow. Laws they recognize to keep order and discipline. As stated previously, the true origins of the Vampires are of myth and of controversy. One common belief is they are cursed demons spawned from an evil source. Destined to roam the earth killing, stalking, and enslaving the weak. This may be true from the perspective of prey, but that is way too easy to accurately depict them. Trying to discover their origins is less important than it is to know their history. It helps explain, why they are, instead of what they are. The earliest confirmed history would tell you that the Vampires lived in the shadow of human existence. The more civilized and discrete of the Vampires harvested farm animals for blood. Pigs, cows, and sheep. Because of their feeding practices, these Vampires tended to live away from humans, on farms and in the mountains. The more vile and vicious Vampires that live in the urban and suburban areas kidnapping the homeless, runaways, forgotten, and loners. They kept them alive and harvested their blood. They considered human blood to be the sweetest and most satisfying. This arrangement was tolerated if the wrong person didn't meet the stated fate. Of course, that's exactly what happened. A decorated war Veteran, drunk and stumbling out of a bar. His way of dealing with his demons. Falls asleep next to a back-alley dive bar. A cover for a group devious Vampire hooligan. Days of tortures, humiliation, and perversions followed. Recorded and posted on the dark web. Eventually going viral. This outraged the general public, inevitably opening up FBI, Congressional, and military investigations. Why the military you ask? Besides the fact that he was a war Vet, he was also the son of a high ranking General. Along with Dr. Brocknar's experiments. That video sparked a war, which helped lead to the beginning of the end to humans as they knew it.

8

HALTING HOSTILITIES

CAJOLE AND ADRINA ARRIVE AT THE BATTLEFIELD. TIRED, DIRTY, and hungry. They see both sides prepared to engage in a violent clash of hate and disdain for one another. Cajole tells Adrina, "We must get to Thanani before she engages Ruby's forces. I just don't know what I'm going to say or do, to convince her to abandon this campaign, regroup, go back to save Goble from the council, then join forces with Roderick to fight the oncoming onslaught.". Adrina replies," You can just leave. Go home to your clan. Forget all this." Cajole says, "Then what? No matter the outcome someone will come looking for me. My family. My clan. Frank, he vampires, Roderick, or Ruby. Worst of all Thanani.". Adrina, reasoning with Cajole says, "We all have an expiration date. I guess it's a matter of how painful that date will be. Gobles said that to me once. He caught me rummaging through his leftover food in the dining hall. I was so distracted by all blood cakes. He grabbed me, picked me up to his eyes. Held me staring, and the first words to me were. "We all have an expiration date, yours is today. Yours will be painful.". Cajole replies, "You know that is the most insightful thing I think I've ever heard you say. Not exactly what you just said to me, but I get it.". Adrina says, "I know. But it's close to the same thing. I spent the next 30 minutes begging for my life and pledging my service to him.". Cajole feeling feisty argues, "I guess it's close, but don't say it's the same quote when it's not.". Adrina feeling just as feisty responds, "It's about the same thing.". Cajole ends the conversation, "Just shut up. we have to get to Thanani.".

They race toward Thanani's war camp on the other side of the battlefield and see Roderick and his wounded warriors heading towards Ruby. Mud alerts the others, "Look! It's Roderick!" Nearly in tears of relief and happiness, Ruby sees the approaching tired and wounded. She aggressively shouts out the order to break formation and surround the weary, "Tend to the wounded! Gather up any needs and nutrients available! The strongest of us to the outer perimeter!" Relieved Roderick exclaims, "You're alive! How did you fare?" Ruby points to her surviving warriors, "What you see is last of us as far as I can tell. Thanani said she sent a kill unit to engage you.". He assures her, "We met no resistance.". Disgusted Ruby replies, "Lying cunt. Mental warfare. I wasn't in time for the most precious of us.". Roderick attempts to comfort and refocus Ruby, "Don't concern yourself with that. We must focus on tending to the injured and getting back to the refuge. What's your situation report?". Ruby gives a quick debrief, "Thanani and her forces are poised to attack. Goble was dragged off the battlefield by the Vampire Nation. They took the vamps with them. I don't know what that indicates. I haven't had much time to analyze the situation. Either way this is a precarious position we're in.". Roderick understanding the landscape says, "The fact that Goble is not here is curious.". Mud approaches Rodrick embraces him as a brother and says, "Well look at the state of you. I guess the gang is all here now.". Before Roderick responds Ruby pulls him away and informs him, "I have to talk to you about Mud.". Mud lightly offended exclaims, "OH, COME ON!".

Thanani sees the changing events unfold and says "Shit! Roderick is back. I guess the best we can hope for is a slow death from one of those Komodo bites.". Gur let's everyone know," I want him at full strength. Where's the glory in killing a wounded mutt?". Sheeba reminds him, "His mind is far more dangerous than his bite my king.". Cajole unintentionally sneaks up on the distracted others. He interrupts their distain, "We all better hope that he and his warriors are healthy, quickly healed, and willing to listen.". Adrina repeats, "Willing to listen.". Thanani, surprised, looks around and replies, "Seeing you here is quite a site. The battlefield is not your forte Cajole. And Adrina? Well, I hope you brought some armor with you as well.". Thorn picks up Adrina to examine her closer, "I'm sure we can strap you somehow to my back, or head, or better yet tail.". "Certainly not! ", Adrina scoffs back. Cajole breaks up the small talk and says, "We must talk.".

Quaid makes it to the Grand Owl's home range. An unusually large grove of massive hickory trees located in the middle of an open plain, about a mile in all directions. Hundreds of these trees tightly grouped together, make a perfect fortress for those who call it their settlement. Here lives a community of owls permanently stationed there strictly to provide security and surveillance. The last line of defense for any oncoming threat to the Grand owl. The Blakiston Fish owls are honored with the task of sacrificing themselves for him. As expected, Quail is met with suspicion and aggression. Centurion tells Quaid, "Your purpose here is expected. The Grand Owl has been waiting for you.". He replies, "Oh! Well, I guess I shouldn't be surprised, but somehow, I am.". The Centurion leads Quaid through a maze of trees, branches, and thorn brushes. A confusing labyrinth designed to delay those who don't belong or have ill intent. One wrong turn and you could be lost for days. Either find yourself back out of the grove, or worst of all, flying into a deathtrap. After a 15 minutes flight they finally arrive at the Grand Owl's living quarters. A large, petrified tree. From what Quaid can see, the tree is fortified as a last stand if all else fails. Grand Owl greets Quaid with a sense of boredom and disinterest." I know why you're here. Do you actually think I would be where I am if I didn't?". Quaid replies, "You do? Well, I guess…". Interrupting, The Grand Owl continues, "If you ever wish to achieve this position, you have a long way to go.". Quaid taken back, remains quiet and listens." Thanani's forces are engaging Roderick's forces. Goble has been apprehended, along with those who follow him. They will all be examined by the way, by the council. They will all be held accountable for their actions. Whether that produces a positive or negative outcome for everyone else.". Quaid urgently tries to inform, "Sir. time is of the essence. I spoke with Cajole and he informed me that there is a massive..." The Grand Owl finishes his thought, "That there is a massive, well-armed fighting force heading in this direction with the intention of enslaving or killing anyone or thing in its path. Led by a psychopathic, murderous primate silverback who calls himself Frank.". An uncomfortable pause occurs what seems to last for hours. "And?", Quaid asks. The Grand Owl understands, "And it's the oldest narrative in history. Someone wants to rule and be worshipped. Along with jealousy and boredom, you have a making for a conqueror. Followed by untimely deaths, misery, destruction, heroic acts, valiancy, and self-sacrifice. Which ultimately leads to myths, legends, heroes, and heroines. This story has been played out a hundred of times over. 80 years was the last to be approximate.". Quaid confused wonders, "Aaannd, what are we going to do?". The Grand Owl responds, "Do what we've always done. Scribe what occurs accurately, when it occurs as accurately, and indifferently as dictated. IT IS NOT OUR JOB TO FORCAST OR PREDICT WHAT IF OR WHAT WILL BE! We are to record as what was. THAT IS ALL! DO. YOU. UNDERSTAND?". Quaid nods his head to reaffirm his commitment and role in the upcoming conflict. Feeling defeated and helpless he turns to return to his post.

The Grand Owl resonates with Quaid's internal conflicts offers insight on what his next steps should be. "If you look to know what is in the future. It is the sloths you seek knowledge from. This I can tell you. Now go with my thoughts of blessing and memory.". Quaid softens the despaired expression on his face and nonverbally receives his instructions. Without further delay Quaid leaves to seek the prognostication of the sloths. It'll be a delaying journey, not agreeable to the time that's needed to benefit the cause, but hopefully a fruitful one. Any bits of intel may be useful in the coming events.

Cajole briefs everyone, "We have a much bigger problem than Roderick." There is an onslaught heading our way. It doesn't take concern to our conflicts. It doesn't take heed to our squabbles or hatred toward Roderick nor the VN or whether we even live or die. All it knows is comply or perish. What I tell you is real, and I've seen it first-hand. He who leads this army knows who you are Thanani. He knows Roderick, He know The Vampire Nation. And he doesn't care.". Adrina repeats, "He doesn't care.". Thanani sits in silence trying to absorb what has been conveyed to her. Everything she planned for. Every scenario she could reenact in her mind has crumbled as time moved on. She doesn't know how to except what she's been told. Cajole is untrustworthy. But this. What does he gain by feeding this information to her? What advantage will he have by lying about this? She cannot think of one.

Gur needs more information, "You're going to have to be more specific.". Cajole continues, "As some may remember, I was sent on a specific mission. To seek and recruit any, and all prospects willing to fight to our cause. My journey east led me to an encampment. An encampment 3 times the size of ours and Roderick's forces combined. While observing the activities, I was captured.". Sheeba surprised says, "Captured? Really?". Cajole catches on to her sarcasm." I was distracted.", he replies. Gur entertained blurts, "Distracted he says.", while looking toward Thorn. Cajole tries to ignore the ridicule he's receiving, "As I said. I was distracted. Consumed by the immense size of said encampment. I was dropped at the feet of the chieftain. A better description would be Commander, who is a silverback.". Thorn says with interest," Silverback you say?". Apprehensive that no-one is taking him seriously Cajole frantically pleads, "As I said, everything I tell you now must be taken with the upmost seriousness. Thanani makes an observation about Cajole's choice of words," It is noted that you're not being sesquipedalian. This would suggest your seriousness in this matter.". He replies, "Correct.". After completely going over all the details, listening ears finally accept the events it hears.

Quaid flies south as fast as he can to travel where the sloths are rumored to be. Mystical animals they are. As the owls are tasked to write accurate history, with little regard for emotion. Strict to their laws. The sloths render no opinion on any matter. Their purpose is to communicate their visions. They are able to tap into frequencies and vibrations that resonates with them more than any other species. They spend their days meditating and interacting with beings from other dimensions, time, and space. Creatures of all kind pilgrimage to them and seek their advice, visions, and knowledge only the sloths are able to tap into. They speak in metaphors and riddles most of the time. The most difficult challenge in interpreting their messages is that you must ask yourself. What does it mean? Who is the message meant for? It is up to the receiver to interpret. Either way, looking back, the sloths are always accurate. Nothing they say should be taking literally. Unless of course somehow it benefits they, who hear it. Precious time is used up every time Quaid stops for rest, food, and assistance in finding the sloths. He has been wrong a half a dozen times while making it to his final destination. Quaid comes across a bloody massacre. Clearly something unusual has occurred here. Something heinous, wicked, and ugly. To say torture and evil lingers everywhere, would only result in linguistic ridicule. This is beyond diabolical. In a small ravine on the edge of an obvious crime scene, there sit a well over 200-pound Jaguar. Unusually large for his species. Licking his wounds and washing himself. Quaid cautiously approaches the large cat knowing that under normal circumstances, Quaid could easily be a meal. He lands on a branch at a safe distance. Quaid greets the cat, "Salve friend.". The Jaguar replies, "There is only one reason why you're here and they're all dead. We did the best we could. I lost close friends of mine in the fight. My sister, my lover, and even my 2 sons. I think the only reason why I'm still alive is to tell the story.". Inquiring further Quaid asks, "What Happened here?". The Jaguar remains reticent and replies, "What happened here needs not to be spoken. I will not be a mode of communication for fear, I won't be a tool to reenforce a mad primate's reputation.". Quaid agrees, "I would guess the story you won't tell, is the same reason why I'm here. What should I call you?". He replies, "My name is Aztec. I was born among the ruins. I pray to them as my own ancestors. They've yet to let me down.". "Fitting", Quaid says, I have to know. Was it Frank?". Aztec explains, "Yes. The Sloths foretold this to me as a cub, but I never meant what it meant till now. How could I? 'Break the back of a silver menace. There you will find your vengeance. And only then will you find peace.', they said to me". Quaid agrees, "Such an ambiguous prophecy. The sloth never makes things easy, do they? Are there any survivors?". "Not that I'm aware of.", Aztec responds. Quaid offers a solution, "If you are to find peace, as the sloths say, I have an opportunity for you to get your vengeance. All I can tell you is the who, when, and where. You already have your why. Eager for revenge Aztec accepts, "That I do. So let our exploits begin then.".

Roderick calls all the Commanders for instructions on the next steps. Thanani and her forces stand in between them and the refuge. They simply can remain stagnant where they are with the injured and running low on supplies and energy. At some point fatigue will set in. That'll lead to frustration and descent. Which in turn will set about doubt in leadership. Ultimately the downfall and demise of all. Even the most hardened warriors curtsy to time. There are no exceptions. The outrage from foregoing events instigates retribution. The last thing Roderick needs is it be directed at him. There has already been rumored rumbling about who is and fault and why are they in this mare's nest.

Roderick begins, "Clearly we need to get back to the refuge. As I see it, we really have 2 options. One, we truculent our way through Thanani, Gur, Thorn, Sheeba and the whole fucking lot of those grims and end this, which I would imagine is the most desirable therapy knowing the ethos of my fellow warriors." Bronze anticipates the other option, "Or a tactical fallback and circle around the long way.". Muscles reacts, "Are you suggesting we retreat?". Baxter follows angrily, "Retreat he says?". Bronze clarifies, "I didn't say we retreat! Don't put words in my mouth.". Muscle replies, "Well, I'm looking right in your mouth horse, and its semantics.". Baxter makes his position known, "RAMS DON'T FUCKING RETREAT NOR FUCKING "FALLBACK"! We are front and centered!". Tank enters the debate, "The rhinos I lead, will follow the burn on my body into the final resting grasslands. I stand with Baxter and his rams.". Bronze, feeling like he's being misunderstood and attacked reminds them, "My stallions are held accountable to this cause and are willing to fight to the death just as much as any of your rams, rhinos or dogs. We have sacrificed and lost just as much as you all have! DO NOT MAKE THE MISTAKE OF BELIEVING THAT WE WILL NOT SCAR OUR BODY FOR A PRINCIPLE HIGHER THEN OUR OWN.". Ruby tries to calm things down, "No-one here does. What say you Strickland?". Strickland offers his thoughts, "We're in an extremely precarious position. I don't care one way or another. Let's make a decision and do it.". Roderick pauses and says, "Okay. We're going to end this one way or another, so let it be here, now."

Roderick stands up with his final words yet spoken. Looking into all his comrades' eyes, knowing the seriousness and conviction of their intentions to finalize the conflict at all costs. He has accepted their decisions as his own and has come to understand that their true sacrifice is to him. They give all for him. He recites their war cry in a show of respect and dedication to them.

Roderick looks at Ruby and says with sincerity, "Loyalty over life." She repeats the word. Then to Muscles, "Loyalty over life." Muscles stands and responds. Roderick looks to the other commanders, "Beauty of Battle, Death from above, GORE! GORE! GORE!, Front and Centered.". Mud stands announcing, "As sweet as Honey.". They all turn to look at Mud. In unison, confirming their commitment to him and initiating a new war cry. They all repeat, "AS SWEET AS HONEY!"

Thanani, visible disturbed, shouts "Shit! We Have them right where we want them. We have an opportunity to FINALLY end this. Decades of struggle come down to this battle. This moment in time. All our losses. All our efforts. All our pain. And now. You are suggesting we forget everything. That somehow, we need them. We make peace with these dogs! WE FORM FUCKING ALLIANCES WITH RODERICK! WITH RUBY? WITH. WITH THE VERY SAME FUCKING SAVAGES THAT WE HUNT?! THIS IS YOUR MESSAGE TO US? TO FIGHT SIDE BY SIDE WITH THESE VERY SAME ANIMALS THAT CAUSED SO MUCH PAIN AND SUFFERING!". Cajole replies, "Yes.". In rage Thanani grabs Cajole, picks him up and threatens to cut his throat. Cajole begs, "I beseech you not to go this route. I am only the messenger. Killing me will not stop what is coming.". Thanani replies," Maybe, but it damn sure will make me feel better.". Sheeba, whispering in Thanani's ear and gently grabbing her wrist says, "I understand sister, let him go. Let him live.".

Thorn asks, "How many summits will we have with them before we actually proceed? I'm ready to kill something." Cajole brushes himself off and says, "You'll have ample opportunity.". Kodi asks," What's next?". Thanani looks around to think, then finally speaks, "What do you suggest Cajole? Since you seem to know it all?". He replies, "I suggest we lay down our aggressions. FOR NOW. We will have to at some point convey this intel to Roderick. Convince him to join forces.". Gur quickly objects, that won't happen!". Cajole continues, "Together we must go to the Vampire Nation's ruins. Show a force of unity. Recruit them, somehow, and prepare for Frank and his army.". Adrina repeats, "Prepare.". Thorn says, "Impossible mission!" Kodi thinks about the past and reminds everyone, "No it's not. War of the spies.". Thanani knows he's right, "War of the spies.". This is the final point that they all agree upon. Kodi says, "History repeats itself every eighty years.".

9

THE EXAMINATION

BACK AT THE VAMPIRE NATION RUINS GOBLE HAS BEEN brought to the Council Hall wearing all white. This is where the head of all the Major and Lesser Families of meaning gather when called for an examination. You can decipher the hierarchy, order of importance, and differences of each family by the size, height, and grandeur of their seats. Generally speaking, the bigger and more dynamic the chair, the more important the member. Lesser heads of families always sit behind never to cross in front while in the Chamber Hall, with the exception of course, in defense and protection to his suzerain. They always arrive to be seated and depart the Hall first. Each Family is Identified by two specific colors. The darker color is always display prominently, while the light color is used as accent. The lesser family colors are reversed to show their fealty. All Families Major, lesser, or any other, wears a black braided lanyard, worn on the left shoulder. This symbolizes their loyalty to the Vampire Nation and the authority to its leader. The most honored and sacred color is black. Gobles is the only member authorized to wear all black. He relinquished his family's colors to dawn the darkest shade. White is seen as a color of disgrace and ridicule in their eyes. It is to be avoided.

Speaking to the head of the council, Henrick, being voted representative to all the major families. Gobles is irate. He yells in Henrick's face, "YOU DARE DRAG ME INTO THIS CONSECRATES HALL POOLED IN WHITE DRABS!?

PLACING SILVER CHAINS ACROSS MY SEATED PODIUM!? YOU HAVE THE AUDACITY TO DO THIS IN FRONT OF THE MASTERS OF YOUR LESSER FAMILIES!? NEED I REMIND YOU THAT YOUR BLACK LANYARDS ..." Henrick talks overs him in reply, "NEED I remind you Gobles. You are charged with serious offenses, warranted offenses, and while you wear those distasteful drabs you hold no position, nor authority or any power that this trial body recognizes. In fact. As I see it, you are the one that needs to show some respect.".

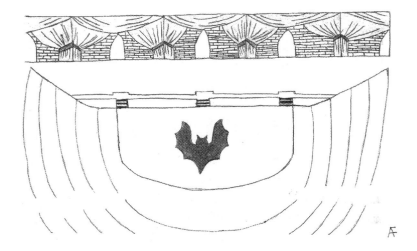

Goble looks around directing his venom at those participating, "This is treason. YOU ALL WILL BE HELD ACOUNTABLE FOR YOUR ROLE IN THIS! YOU ALL WILL BE EXAMINED! Those loyal to me, as well as my native family, will seek justice for this outrageous trial.". Unconcerned with his threats, Henrick replies, "Those loyal to you have been arrested for examination themselves. They have much more to worry about then your well-being. And as for your Native family? As you know, they are forbidden to take part in this examination and must except the decision of its conclusion. Or be subject to their own perusal.". Scuffing Gobles says, "These examinations are a farce. I would imagine the verdict is already established and this is just a formality.". Henrick suggests, "Perhaps. But if that is what you truly believe. Then why not save us all the pantomime, confess to your transgressions, and perform Felo-de-se. Self-sentencing. For the betterment of our nation.".

Goble directs his words to the head of all the families," I do not hold you all personally responsible. I understand that you have been compelled to take such extreme actions. I do not and will not hold this against you. This I promise. I will not hold you all responsible if you stand up and put an end to this now. However, if this treason, and that's exactly what this is. Treason. If this mutiny goes on unchallenged and you refuse to honor your oaths. You leave me no alternative but to seek my own justice upon you. Your families, your lesser vassals. You will be remembered for generations to come as an example of the consequences of a traitor's disloyalty and disobedience.". While looking at Henrick, "This is my promise to you Henrick. You get no such courtesies. You are already staked. I will not show you any mercy. Your name, likeness, and the very fangs that feed your life force will be cemented into these very walls. So that in a thousand years, future generations will know exactly what a treasonous whore looks like. You will be the standard.".

Goble extends his fangs and bites into his forearm siphoning a mouthful of his own rotted blood. He stares at all the heads of families to get photographic images of all of them and their corresponding sigils, colors, and lesser vassals. He spews out a rancid mixture of blood and venom onto the chamber's floor in their direction, landing on and covering the Vampire Nation's universal symbol, a red bat. This final act of defiance displays the seriousness of his promise. Most members of the lesser families looked on in fear and shock. Hissing and murmuring incoherent curses under their breaths. The heads of the major families looked to Henrick for his reaction. They received none.

Just and sarcastic smirk, then signs of annoyance. Henrick stands up staring at Goble. Henrick orders his guards, "Take our most exalted leader to his secured living arrangements to await the coming examination.".

The Hyenas elect a leader. He is unlike any other before him. Disgruntled over the years of the low status of the hyenas and wild dogs are held to. Being looked down to, years of servitude and ridicule has left him bitter and spiteful. Longing for the days his species recognizes the potential power they yield when directed to a common purpose. Always focused on the future and what could be when given the opportunity to act. He sees this new leadership position, as a chance to begin a new era. An era of renewed strength in his species. Azizi presents himself to Thanani as the new Hyena/wild dog commander.

Azizi wears sharpened steel armor to cover his claws, similar to gloves. In close combat, He attempts to gauge out his enemy's eyes before finishing them off. He prefers light body armor that allows for easy mobility and speed. His body is covered more with small stripes rather than spots with longer pointed ears. From the back of his neck to his tail, Azizi's spine is decorated with longer, bushy hair that stands up to give an aggressive posture. Azizi introduces himself, "I am Azizi, the elected leader..." Thanani interrupts him, "Took long enough for your..." Azizi stands his ground by finishing his thoughts, "AS I WAS SAYING! THERE WILL A NEW ATTITUDE within the ranks of we hyenas and wild dogs. As I speak, all my kind is being reintroduced with the art of war, beginning with discipline. We will hold up our end of the alliance. The weakest of us are being put to the sword as the others watch. I understand this weakens our numbers temporarily, but in the long run it will strengthen our clan and in turn strengthen us all as a fighting unit. The execution of our weakest will stand as a reminder and motivator to those who fail. Would you agree?". Thanani agrees," Long overdue in my opinion.". Azizi continues, "I would further add. Once this transformation is complete, my brethren will not be humiliated or in contempt as in days past.". Gur inquires, "And when would you expect all this transformation be completed? When are we not expected to laugh at your clan's failures?". Azizi confidently replies," Right here. Right now." Sheeba is pleased, "Good. We will hold you accountable for your people's mistakes from now on.". Azizi replies, "As it should be.". Cajole speaks up, "Good cause we cannot afford any weak links.". Adrina repeats, "Any. weak. links.". Cajole and Adrina begin arguing, he tells her, "Can you stop doing that? Repeating the last things, I say!". She replies, "I'm just trying to emphasize the importance of what you said.". Cajole replies, "I know you are! But you are a teeny, little mole rat with a squeaky voice. And when you do that, the opposite effect happens. It makes what mine, or anyone else's words sound ridiculous and less important. No offense.", Adrina reasons, "I'm just trying to add weight to the...". "SHUT UP!", Cajole blurts.

Thanani refocuses the group, "Ladies and Gentlemen. We have a serious dilemma presented before us. If what Cajole says is true, and I don't doubt it. Then we must make peace with our centuries old sworn enemies in one hand. And in the other, we wait and deal with an even greater threat of which we know nothing about.". Sheeba gives her opinion, "I say we fight with what we have in front of us and deal with the new threat when that presents itself.". Thorn seconds the notion, "I like that! That is a solid plan.". Cajole offers another alternative, "Let me plant this seed if I may. What is our ultimate goal here? To survive. To live in peace. To go about our business daily without persecution. To go about raising our families unmolested. Am I right?". He pauses to let in sink in for a moment. "So why must we fight now? Here? Are we too prideful that we cannot lay our arms down and compromise? If later, we cannot come to an accord with Roderick or any of his forces, then so be it. But why do any of us have to NEEDLESSLY fight and die right here, right now?". Gur convinced," He makes a good point.". Bandit says, "So we will need a neutral party. A mediator to speak on our behalf. Do We Have one?" Cajole replies, "Yes we do. An owl named Quaid. In my travels back to warn you, I encountered a young owl. He assured me he would go talk to the Grand Owl. If he were to intervene, surely Roderick, Ruby, and the whole lot of them would respect the Grand owl's words.". Thanani disagrees, "That'll never happen. I have had my run ins with the Grand Owl. He has one purpose, one mind set, one mission. He'll never deviate from it. He is the most dedicated of his kind and will go to his grave not swayed by any circumstance.". Cajole says, "Then we just leave.". Kodi, outraged at the thought exclaims, "LEAVE? And look like cowardly fools?".

Cajole argues the point, "It really doesn't matter what we look like. We must get the support of Goble and the Vampire Nation. We can start there.". Thanani makes her mind up, "That is what we'll do then. You better be right on this Cajole. Commanders, prepare your troops to make the journey back to the ruins.".

Muscles notices the ever-changing battlefield. He alerts Roderick," Look! Thanani and her forces are leaving the field of battle. What in the fuck pile is going on?". Roderick assesses, "I'm not sure but stay alert and ready yourselves for a surprise attack. Do you think this is a trap?". Ruby replies, "Can never say for sure with her." Mud excited reminds everyone, "This is our opportunity to get back to the refuge!". Strickland takes to flight with a flock of his best observers. They circle above them get a better picture of their intentions. Roderick orders him to report frequently on all troop movements. Ruby, suspicious, thinks to herself," *What the fuck are they up to? They had us exactly where they wanted us.*". Roderick barks out directions, "Prepare Your warriors to make haste back home to the refuge. We move in 10 mikes!".

As Roderick and his forces cautiously begin their march back to the refuge, the wolf moon begins to make its effects known. In times of peace, it acts as a powerful aphrodisiac. Perfect time for breeding. Not so much for other unsuspecting species who happen to be in the sexual collateral damage crosshairs. It's best to stay clear during this time or, be made a victim of their aggressive passion. The terriers being the most common receiver of such advances. However, when planned at the right time, the wolf's moon is an effective battle tool. It amplifies faster healing amongst the Weres and strengthens them tenfold. At least that's what it appears to do. No-one knows exactly why or how it works. The Weres feed off its energy. The effect of injury is numbed. Blood thirst sets in. Some Weres go into such a kill frenzy, they drop dead from exhaustion. Therefore, most commanders set their battle plans around it's rising. But for ever pro there is a con. During the wolf moon it is very difficult to manage and control the Weres. Similar to the great Viking berserker. The one thing a great battlefield commander understands is maneuverability. They understand that battlefield situations change. They recognize that they must adapt to the enemy and effectively respond. During the wolf moon this is almost impossible. Only the most disciplined and battle tested Weres can comprehend, reorganize, rethink, adapt, and adjust. This all must be considered in the calculations when planning an attack during this time. The other species understand this and adapt accordingly. The wolf moon has made its presence known.

As Thanani and her forces exit the theater of battle, they notice the rising of the wolf moon. She urges her army to move faster. In the distance she can hear the howling echo. It isn't fear that grabs this moment. Fear hasn't been a part of her psyche since she was a young cub. No. Her concern is the unnecessary loss to her army now that she has lost the tactical advantage. She also understands the howling is a call to arms and gathering for all other werewolf clans to unite. Thanani and her forces are now surrounded by pockets of fanatical Were clans looking to fuck or kill anything in their path. She can hear she is surrounded. Roderick heads toward the refuge with speedy pace. The youngest and least experienced warrior wereswolves stop. They begin to grow bigger, angrier, more intense. The effects of the wolf moon fill their spirit with rage. Their focus turns to the rear guard of Thanani's caravan.

Ruby yells to Roderick," I'm sure you're aware of the current state!". Roderick explains, "There's not much I'm going to be able to do to contain this. If our Weres attack them. It'll be a useful sacrifice keeping Thanani occupied if this is a trap and buying us needed time to get back home. Hopefully, this will damage a good portion of her army.

Before another word could be spoken the 20 Weres, effected by the wolf moon, charge toward the rear guard, mainly made up of the newly trained Hyenas with Azizi in command. Azizi organizes and presses his troops into action, "FORM A LINE TWENTY ACROSS! FOUR DEEP! SEND WORD TO THANANI, We WILL HOLD THIS LINE!".

Sheeba orders two of her closest sisters to reinforce the flanking sides. The Weres charge forward with ill intent. Crashing, clawing, biting, and killing. The lioness sisters make the most of their opportunity to repel when the situation dictates, but inevitably fall back to formation. Weres leap into Azizi's third and fourth line, only to meet death and their final battle. The effects of the wolf moon have lived up to its reputation. Those who live to speak of their survival, will present it as a badge of honor. "Surviving the wolf moon" is always used as a bragging point. As the Hyena lines weaken and evaporate from the skirmish, so do the Weres. When last of them have been killed off, Azizi, the lioness sisters, and fifteen Hyenas are the only ones that remain standing. This gives Roderick and his warriors enough time to get back to the refuge, even if there was a trap waiting for them. Azizi has proven himself invaluable to Thanani in the upcoming tribulations. Battle torn; he takes the surviving members back to the ruins far behind the main army.

The Examination begins with Henrick reading out loud in the sacred chamber. He informs the head of all the major and lessor families the charges being brought forth. "Gobles, you are charged with the following crimes against the Vampire Nation and it's families. 1. Treason 2. Conspiracy to commit domestic Terrorism against the families. 3. Unauthorized War of Declaration. 4. Mutiny. 5. Coercion. and finally, showing weakness in the face of the enemy, widely known as COWARIDE! How to your plea?". Goble formally enters his plea, "Not guilty. Not guilty on all accounts.". Henrick continues, "Then let us begin, shall we? Good. As you know, everyone here in our sacred chambers can provoke a thought or question. They will identify the family they represent, and you will acknowledge their lineage in return. They all will have an opportunity to ask one question or make one statement. When all members have concluded their say then you will have an opportunity for final closure. The chamber will deliberate, and every head of family will cast their vote of guilt or innocent in this chamber for all to see.". Impatiently Gobles demands, "Get on with it already!". Henrick begins," As you wish. I am Henrick of Family Von Henlock, and elected head authority of the Vampire Council.". There is a pause, waiting for Goble's acknowledgement. Goble nobs his head in recognition.

Henrick asks, "Did you not make war plans, then carry them out against Roderick and his forces without the consent of this council's knowledge and authority, receiving your orders from Thanani? And need I remind or inform this examination body, that Thanani is not a member of the Vampire nation.". Goble clarifies, "Well which question would you like me to answer? Clearly your question is in fact six questions, consolidated and combined into one.".

Henrick confidently states, "It doesn't matter. You can pick the one that you feel is less... Hm? Incriminating? The reality is the answer will all be the same." Goble replies, "No.". "Interesting.", Henrick sarcastically mumbles. The next Vampire Head of Family speaks, "Droskon of family Voldimote. Do you possess the tactical knowledge to engage in an effective campaign to defeat Roderick and his forces?". Annoyed Gobles answers, "I believe I do.". Next voice echoes, "Alearick of major family Bornbrick. Did you threaten every family with heliacal punishment if they did not bend to your command?". Gobles answers, "Yes, I did. I did for the betterment of ...". Henrick cuts him off, "WHO ARE YOU TO DICTATE TO THIS COUNCIL WHAT IS BEST FOR OUR...". Gobles quiets Henrick, "AND YOU HAVE HAD YOUR OPPORTUNITY TO ADDRESS THE FLOOR WITH YOUR ONE QUESTION! As I've stated. We are at war. I did not have the luxury of time to debate war tactics, plans, approvals, or repudiation. I needed to seize the moment. And I needed the assistance of an accomplished commander and fighter. I did what was needed.". After a moment of intense silence. It was broken with another question, "Fron of lesser family Plexidor vassal to major family Plexidus. Did you take our finest warrior to battle without the consent of the council?". "Yes, I did.", Gobles answers. Having had enough, "Lexor of family Plexidus. Why are we here? Is this not a waste of our nightlight? For centuries we have fought the Weres and their allies. We have used any resources necessary as a means to an end. I grow tired of such spectacle. I have a domain to govern. For all I care, Goble can go wage war against any species not of the Vampire Nation. I will retrieve my armed stewards as well as lesser family, to make haste to my realm. I urge all of you to do the same.".

Goble snickers as he watches the Plexidus and Plexidor members make their leave. Henrick is visibly indignant. It is an unwelcomed event, and he calls for a respite to regroup and reorganize the examination. He orders the guards to secure Gobles back to his holding cell. As Gobles sits in his living cell eating blood bread. He can see the departure of the Plexidus convoy in the distance. But there is something is wrong. There appears to be a war party out in the distance. At first, he thinks to himself, *Thanani has returned to release him from his captivity. Did she eliminate the likes of Roderick and Ruby? Can the final battle be over? Ultimate victory perhaps?".* The rising of the sun at dawn makes it difficult and unclear to see the oncoming party. Then he thinks, "*Why does the size of these beasts seem unusually big?"*

10

BACK AT THE REFUGE

QUAID AND AZTEC FLY, SWIM, TRUDGE, AND HASTEN THEIR WAY north. Overcoming their own physical and mental challenges. Ignoring hunger. Stopping for a break to rehydrate and feed at opportune moments. Minimal sleep has taken its toll. At a small water hole, they take a quick stop to gather their thoughts. Aztec says, "So where exactly are we heading. I know north, generally speaking, but where specifically?" Quaid replies, "Haven't really thought about it. I guess I just figured when we get closer, we'd start with the first people we came across that made sense. That would be the Wolf's refuge. The first destination we'll come across. It's the southernmost stronghold that'll hopefully receive us. There's only one problem, you. You're a grim.". "Me? Why am I the one problem? And what a grim?", Aztec replies defensively. Quaid explains, "A feline? Cat? That's what they call your kind. Weres and Terriers have been at war in the region we're traveling to, they have been at war for as long as I can remember.". Aztec feeling offended says, "And? Their war has nothing to do with me.". Quaid explains, "That may not matter. Roderick, Ruby, Muscles, the union of species will still mistrust you and see you as the enemy, they may try to kill you.". Defeated Aztec asks, "Great! So, what's plan B?". "Well, we can bypass them, try to find Thanani and her allies. I'm quite sure you'd be welcomed there. Only problem is, where to find her? The Vampire Ruins would be my first guess, but the Vampires aren't much of a welcoming committee. If she isn't there, there's no telling how we will be received. We're not far from the refuge. I could go ahead. I will be received and secure your safety. If I can guarantee your safe passage with Roderick, then you will have nothing to worry about.". Aztec replies, "Well isn't this just rich? And If not?". Quaid says, "Then it's a more than likely chance, that the last thing you'll see. Is your throat being torn out?", Aztec kiddingly responds, "Oh! Lovely, exactly what I wanted to experience more than anything."

Roderick makes it back to the refuge. Relieved but still on high alert for traps or ambushes. His recon force clears out all areas in a one-mile radius and organizes sentry post lookouts. He orders the immediate attention to those most injured, then calls for all his fellow leaders. As he and Ruby take a moment to reminisce and review the past events, he hears a noise coming from infamous holding pit. He calls for the blood pack, Mud, Muscles, and Strickland to join him. Cautious of it being a trap, Strickland flies over to inspect the pit's content. Surprised, he yells to Roderick, "It's a Bear". Upon hearing this, Mud immediately runs over for a closer look. Mud, excited, points into the pits contents and yells, "HA! It is a bear everyone! Well, how the hell did you get in there? Wait, I know her! Well maybe it's not ok. This girl is a tough one. At least that's her reputation.". Roderick and his comrades walk over to look inside the pit. A lone female Kodiak bear. Weary, dirty, and not happy. She speaks to them, "So, I'm assuming that since I'm looking up at you fuckers, that Thanani lost the battle, and I will be joining her and her consiglieres shortly. Or as this pit has its reputation, not so shortly." Mud overzealous shouts, "Nope. You're wrong. SHERRIAN! But we didn't either. Both sides just kind of went their own ways.". Sherrian replies, "I know you, Mudawarr! I know you for being an idiot.". Feeling special for being recognized Mud replies, "Thank you. For knowing me, not for knowing me as an idiot. Obviously. But it does feel good having a reputation that precedes me. Just not that of an idiot.". Ruby interrupts, "Damn, you're in a tough spot down there sister.".

Sherrian aggravated with her situation replies, "I'm not your sister, wolf-bitch. And are you going to share that honey Mudawarr?" Mud dismisses her, "This? Why should I? I mean, you are the enemy. You did fight against my benefactor did you not? Yes, you did. So why would I share my honey, honey. HAHAHHA!". Sherrian unamused, "Puns, really? I'll tell you why. When our contracts are expired, and we see each other back at Spider Stream. If I get out of here, I'm going to destroy you! NOW SEND SOME HONEY DOWN HERE!". Mud ignores her cries and continues eating clumsily, spilling his honey on his lap. Giggling at a joke he rewinds in his mind over and over. Sherrian changes her attitude and uses a different strategy, "I'm sorry. Could you please share your honey or get me something to eat?". Mud satisfied replies, "Thaaaat's better. You have such an amazing attitude. This is why I love you. If I knew you.". Mud tosses what's left of his vice and quietly observes her eagerly eating. Everyone leaves. Mud stays to further the conversation and says," You know what I was just thinking? You're going to be my lady-bear, aren't you? I mean, this is how all the fairytale stories start and play out don't they? Damsel in distress. You! Huge warrior hero swoops in to save the day. Me. At first there's no connection, but then, At some weird uncomfortable pause, but at a totally appropriate time. We kiss. *Then comes marriage, then cubbies in the cubby carriage.*". Sherrian disgusted says, "Are you insane?". Mud envisioning their future together continues, "It's so true. We're going to have these huge wholly bear mammoths! Just so you know, we're going to need like a, like a. Lake filled with fishies and honey. Oh! TONS of berries. Raspberry, blueberry, cherries, and blackberries. I call them black bearberries. HA! You'll see. I'll ask the first sloth from the south I run into.". Sherrian confirms her notion, "Yup, you're insane. I'm not having yours, or anyone else's cubs for that matter. I'm not even going to allow anyone to get close to me in that way. NOPE, NOT HAPPENING!". Changing the subject Mud asks, "So don't you want to know what happened?". Sherrian replies, "Why do I have a feeling that you're going to tell me anyway, no matter what answer I give?".

Mud begins to tell the details, "So, Roderick and I went to the see the Komodo to find out what happened to Dustin, a messenger greyhound. Turns out the Komodos killed him. Mainly because he was crossing through their territory. Then I helped organize a revenge attack on them, but I couldn't stay for the battle because I had to run back to save the younglings with Ruby. We get back and thwart the attack, but we were too late. The baby species met their maker, but we were able to save some. But then we were surrounded. Hyenas, tigers, lions, vampires. Bears of course but you knew that. And racoons. Ready to exterminate us all. But then we had a parlay. Kodi lied about me, there was a little skirmish, two rhinos tackled me down. Took all their strength by the way. Ruby tried to cut my throat because she thought I was a traitor. Oh, the head Vampire got carted away by his people for an examination. The Hyenas made assess out of themselves. Roderick finally arrived with the wounded. I prepared everyone for the finally battle but Thanani took her forces and left. So, I figured this would be a perfect time to pack our shit and high tail it back here. But then, the wolf moon made its presence felt. Some of the younger Weres lost their minds and attacked Thanani's rear guard and we were like fuck that let's go! Eventually made it back here to see you down there begging for some honey.

Sherrian and Mud stare at each other for a minute waiting for the other to say the next words. Sherrian breaks the silence, "That's it?". Mud replies, "That's about it.". Sherrian ready to move on asks, "Well, what does a girl need to do to get out of this pit? Mud answers, "I couldn't say for sure. You'd have to run that past the wolves. I'm quite sure, your freedom isn't a priority for them right now. What got you in there in the first place?".

Sherrian regretfully replies, "Love for my children. Revenge. I was living peacefully and alone. On the outskirts of Spider stream.

A group of members lead by the blood pack decided to make a training session of me and my cubs. They were tough I must admit. But when it was all said and done, I lost the life of my cubs. Three of them suffered the same fate. I killed three of those bastards. If it weren't for the other bears from Spider Stream coming to my aid, I may be with my cubs right now. Knowing the mental suffering from the trauma this caused, maybe I should have traveled to the afterlife with my cubs. Anyway, I declared a blood feud against all Wolves. And Terriers as well. The terriers, just because they resemble them.". Mud says, "Well I for one, am glad it played out the way it did. If it hadn't, I wouldn't have a future life partner, right?". Sherrian defiantly, "Wrong! If I ever get out of here, I am heading right back to Spider Stream and forgetting all this.". "If.", Mud reminds her.

Huddled up and analyzing their security and next moves; Roderick speaks to his commanders, "Strickland, Send your scouts out and recon our position for threats. I plan on reducing the threat level so our warriors can recover some.". Strickland flies understanding his orders. "Copy that.". Roderick turns to the others, "If things seem to at ease up some, I plan on the issuing orders to make sludge." Ruby agrees, "The sludge? Sounds like a great plan. They need to lose themselves for a while.". Roderick continues, "Well, it's a start. The sludge will at the very least help them connect to their ancestors. Give them guidance and support.". Ruby adds, "As shall we meet ours.". All the commanders are pleased with the prospects of winding down for period of time to reflect on recent events and honor their lost and living compatriots.

Grand Owl Boris-

It is hard to accurately describe what sludge is. In the simplest terms, sludge is an extremely potent liquid hallucinogen. Consumed orally. Meant primarily

to connect with those closest to those who drink it.
Made from a rare plant found only in the coldest
most secluded regions of North America. Words
can't describe the euphoria those that drinks it feel,
but it takes days to recover from its effects. Some
describe it as pure love and tranquility. A place to
learn and grown with their ancestors. Others say it
is your deepest desires. Everyone agrees, they don't
ever want to come out of this state on consciousness.
Fortunately, there isn't much of it to last. Everyone
would be addicted to it.

Strickland returns with Quaid in his claws then drops him at Roderick feet. Quaid breathing heavy from fright freezes and braces himself, anticipating bodily harm. Strickland reports, "Roderick, we captured this little owl approaching our refuge in haste. He does have tale to tell. With a very interesting companion, he apparently wants us to accommodate. Roderick reassures Quaid's safety, helps him to his feet, and brushes random debris stuck between his feathers, "Little bird. What brings you to our refuge? And who is this companion Strickland speaks of?" Quaid relieved of his survival; "I am Quaid. I was raised and trained to oversee the midlands. The region between here and the ruins of the vampires. During my observances I came across a small mole rat and fox. They seemed quite desperate to talk to Thanani. He claimed of a threat from the east named Frank. A bloodthirsty silverback gorilla. This silverback has the backing over 10,000 warriors. He also conveyed to me that the Vampire Council has seized Goble for an examination. I traveled to notify the Grand Owl, but he already knew the details. This led me to seek the advice of the sloths. And here's the part I need you to order a safe passage."

Roderick replies, "That would be Cajole and Adrina if my information is accurate. This would explain a lot. Go on.". Quaid continues," I arrived to where the sloths should have been. That is where I met my traveling companion. He will be able to continue this story. You will have to order his safe passage." Roderick grants his request and orders all his forces to stand down and allow a safe passage to Quaid's friend. Quaid adds, "His name Is Aztec. His warriors were slaughtered by this silverback named Frank. He apparently killed off all the sloths. He has come with me to tell his story, and he's a mountain lion.". Outrage ensues, Muscle loses his temper lounges to grab Quaid but misses. He looks to Roderick," A mountain lion!! We are giving a grim safe passage?" Quaid defends his comment, "He takes no part in the feud between you, Thanani or the Vampire Nation, I'm not sure he's ever encountered a bear before.". Disturbed at what she hears whispers in Roderick's ear, "This isn't good.".

Roderick analyzes the situation and says, "This sole mountain lion poses no threat to us or this refuge. Take the blood pack with you and retrieve this grim named Aztec. We will hear what he has to say. Strickland, your crew will provide overwatch. Muscles, have your warriors provide extra security. Designate a path straight to our meeting grounds. If this mountain lion shows any signs of aggression, I order an immediate death sentence on him. And this owl.".

Tensions are high. Quaid leads the Blood pack, led by Muscles, to the area that Aztec was hiding. With tensions high, the blood pack escorts Aztec back to the meeting grounds. Surrounded by snapping terriers, laughing rhinos, and the indifferent rolling eyes of the stallions. Aztec, annoyed by the overreaction and hostile pageantry, finally sits down to talk to Roderick and his forces.

In a low, passive tone, Aztec introduces himself, "First let me just say. I am not a mountain lion. Ok? Technically, I am a Jaguar. Secondly, I know nothing of this Thanani, Gur, Vampire Nation, or any of you as a matter of fact, aside from what Quaid has told me. I am not here to join, spy on, fight for, or anything else anyone may have in mind for me. I am here for one reason, and one reason only. To get some FUCKING PAYBACK!". The Blood Pack jump to their feet and ready themselves in a fighting stance. Aztec realizing what he has triggered, pauses, and lowers his tone. He continues, "To get some payback on this fucking cunt that calls himself Frank.". Roderick replies, "I can't honestly say that I've never encountered a Jaguar before. At the very least I wouldn't be able to say that tomorrow. And what of this Frank? I've never heard this name before Quaid here and you. Why would I need to be any more afraid of him then the VN, Thanani, or any other threat we've had to thwart off? By the way, why should I take your word on this and trust you, a cat?". Aztec says, "Well, I actually don't give a shit what you believe or don't believe. Even whether or not you're scared of Frank and his plans to destroy you. I only care about killing him. By any means necessary. Now if I can get help to expedite this then awesome, but if not, I'll be on my way if you please. Tank starts to laugh, get comfortable, you're not going anywhere, anytime soon cat.

Aztec and Quaid continue to tell their stories and gain the curiosity of Roderick and his commanders. He orders Tank and the Blood Pack to take Aztec to the pit and join Sherrian for safe keeping.

Roderick speaks to his commanders, "I understand that he is a cat, and he may be untrustworthy. I get that. We must take everything under consideration here. Quaid vouches for him. Have we ever known an Owl to lie before?". Muscles quickly reminds, "War of the spies?". Roderick acknowledges," Agreed but besides that. Would this Owl betray us?". Has anyone here ever seen his species before? Why would a Jaguar travel this far, put his own life at risk to talk to us? For what? Unless what he says is true. Strickland, you said your scouts saw nothing for at least a 100-mile radius, correct?". Strickland reports, "Nothing we need to worry about boss.". Roderick opens the floor for input, "Then I tend to believe him. All your thoughts?" Ruby immediately speaks, "I'm thinking on the same lines as you. He apparently has no connection with Thanani or the Vampire Nation.". Muscle interjects, "Roderick. You know how I feel about any feline. I will fight along you through hell, you know that. Don't ask me to trust that cat.". Bronze gives his opinion, "I don't care. Just tell me who, what, when, and how. Are we still having the sludging?". Tank laughs at the stallion, "HAHA! Idiot. I'm ok with whatever you decide Rick." Roderick turns his thoughts to muscles, "I'm not asking you to trust him Muscles. But what are your thoughts on what he said?". Muscle replies, "Well that will entail me trusting him. I don't believe him. It's going to take more convincing. Much more.". Baxter, not to be left out adds, "I'm in, whatever the gameplan."

Roderick makes a temporary decision, "This is what I purpose. We will have our sludging...". "YES!", Bronze yells out. Roderick continues, "We will have our sludging tomorrow night. We'll let our ancestors decide our next steps. Then reconvene with better insight two nights thereafter. Once the effects have completely worn off. AYE?" Ruby, "Aye.". Strickland, "Aye.". Tank, "Aye.". They all turn to look at Muscles, "Aye.". Baxter, "Aye.". Bronze losses himself in the excitement yells, "AYE MOTHER FUCKERS! LET THE SLUDGING BEGIN!"

Back at the pit Mud, Sherrian, and Aztec continue their conversation. Everyone is in a frenzy of jubilee preparing for the sludging. There is an air of excitement spreading rapidly as word gets passed around. You can hear rumbling of all the possibilities and scenarios those will and won't find themselves in. Stallions telling the rhinos that they plan on molesting them. Eagles shitting on Terriers from an altitude of a thousand feet. Even one brave terrier threatening to make Ruby his bitch for the night. An unlikely event that would cost him his life. This is a time of celebration. An opportunity to release rage and love. Pent up energy and anger for past regrets. A time to honor the fallen and reconnect with ancestors for advice. The sludge effects species and being differently. By the end of the calamity, there always is a lesson to be learned.

Aztec hears the commotion, "What's going on up there?". Mud replies, they're preparing for the sludging.". Sherrian distressed, "Oh damn! Here we go. Am I going to have to endure this? Get me out of here so I can go home.". Aztec asks, "What's the big deal?". Sherrian explains, "Trust me. Once this circus gets on the road. It's a real shit show. You want to talk about a disaster?". Mud helps, "It's a lot a fun Aztec. You drink this rancid liquid, then give it about 20 minutes. BOOM! THE NONSENSE BEGIN-ITH! You meet you ancestors, act up. I mean you're in such a state of bliss you have no idea what the fuck is happening. And anything goes.".

Aztec agrees, "Sounds like the festivals where I come from. They are a lot of fun. Are you participating Mud?". Mud happily replies, "Damn shit I am!". Aztec requests, "Think you can get some for me? I want to try.". Mud replies, "Absolutely. Sherrian care for a schwig". Sherrian declines, "No! Keep that shit away from me! I take a sip of that crap and the next thing you know I'll be mating with some rhino. Or even worse, I may get too slugged and end up mating with you mud. Have a cave full of cubs and must look at your ugly mug through my kids every day. Mud deviously replies, "Then I'm definitely making sure that you get your share.".

Mud scurries off yelling." HURRY UP WITH THAT FUCKING SLUDGE! I GOT CUBBIES TO MAKE YOU WRETCHED HEATHENS!" Sherrian and Aztec make themselves comfortable knowing they aren't going anywhere for at least a few days. They exchange each other's chronicles realizing that their experiences are quite familiar to each other. Quaid flies to the pit and informs Aztec," I've been granted permission to leave and go back to the Grand Owl's home range. Hopeful, with these recent events, I can get the Grand Owl to reconsider. I wish you a safe journey wherever it may lead you.". Aztec replies, "As I do you, my friend. Hope to see you again soon.".

11

THE SLUDGING

ALL PREPARATIONS HAVE BEEN MADE FOR THE SLUDGING. ANYONE who doesn't want to partake in the festivities will be put on post and given a special meal to keep them satisfied throughout the duration. Afterwards, they will be allowed to rest and enjoy whatever their vice is for two days. A small reward or compensation for their self-sacrifice so others may be given the chance to unwind and enjoy themselves. As for the participants, impatience and excitement sets in. There will be a small ceremony and honor to everyone's gods. Once the bonfire is lit, it will provoke small bonfires to follow. At that point anyone is free to indulge in the sludge.

Roderick addresses the impatient participates, "Tonight. We honor those who have given their lives so we may celebrate and live on. May our gods watch over us tonight and give us their blessings. May our ancestors embrace us with their warm loving hearts and give us the wisdom to better ourselves. LIGHT THE FIRE AND LET THE SLUDGING COMMENCE!

An honored warrior from each species carries a torch over to a massive pile of wood that looked as if a forest of trees were cut to make it. They were soaked with a highly flammable liquid, fermented leftovers from concocting the sludge. The warriors throw their firesticks into the middle, setting off a massive conflagration seen a mile away. This provokes the other smaller beacons to be set off. From a distance, it looks as if a hundred lanterns are lit to light the night into a blaze.

The Stallions are the most eager to start drinking and lead the festivities. Almost immediately, led by Bronze, all the horse start bucking, neighing, and mounting each other. Changing form from horse to human and back again. The Rams aren't far behind. Overly eager to meet their worshipped god Ares, they ensure they are fully armored. In the Ram's eyes, it is the ultimate disrespect to be received by their deity without their war regalia. The Rams consume their intoxication then fall to formation.

The Weres and Terriers rip their body armor and clothing off anticipating the effects from the sludge. They change from human form to animal incarnation and begin howling into the sky. Drool pouring from between their teeth and out of their mouths, they start sizing each other up for a ritual of the Alpha males. Fighting for position in the pack. The younger of them testing the elders for the rights to lead. Roderick and Ruby are no exception. They have held their position for years and if either submit, the direction of their species and the whole war machine could easily head in a different direction.

The size of the Rhinos dictate that they get double portion. For the most part they look forward to meeting their ancestors. They look to them for approval, advice, and ultimately comfort. They long to re-experience the love remembered from their loved ones. To present themselves as a proud legacy to those that came before them. Strickland and his raptors are the last to indulge. They see the sludging as an opportunity to advance their arial skills. Maneuvers that would otherwise never be attempted, due to the extremely high probability of death or injury. The raptors would spend the duration perfecting dives and arial agility pattern, weaving in and out of tight corners and spaces. As well as hazing the other species. Agitating them, provoking, and hoping for a response.

Mud goes to get his portion of sludge. He grabs extra servings for the captures in the pit. Excited for the coming experiences, he drops their servings down to them urging them to partake. Aztec willingly obliges and consumes his sludge without hesitation. Sherrian has her reservations and pushes it aside. Mud drinks his then sits back waiting for the sludge's effect to take hold.

Random Stallion explodes, "I can fucking feel the rush! Who dares me to go over to one of those rams and mount him like one of the horniest little mares in heat?". The others laugh and begin the ritual of sarcastically doubting him to provoke the intended action. Another Stallion replies, "I'll go mount one of those fucking rhinos!". Soon enough, all the stallions start trying to out-do the others. Random Stallion blurts, "I'll go find Gur, grab him by his fucking mane, and ass-blast him till he coughs up baby horse lion furballs!"

All the other broncos start laughing out loud. One replies," What in the hell would that look like?" Other shouts out, "Imagine a horse's body, a lion's mane and little lion cock!" Everyone burst out in uncontrollable laughter. Another stallion threatens to impale a Terrier and turn him into an old fashion corndog. This continues until one of the stallions gains the others attention and says, "Watch this shit." In the distance he sees a group of rhinos unaware of the impending shenanigans. He nonchalantly walks over to an unsuspecting rhino from behind. The all others see what's unfolding but say nothing. They are just as eager to see how things transpire as much as the stallions do. Things start to get quiet as the deed is about to happen. Before the victim can realize the situation, the stallion, in human form, jumps on the rhinos back, wraps a rope around the rhino's face and into his mouth. He starts bucking in an attempt to fling off the stallion. "LOOK AT ME BOYS! I'M MAKING THIS RHINO MY BITCH!" Everyone starts counting down from 10 seconds. 10, 9, 8, 7, 6. The rhino frantically begins bobbing his head up and down after hearing someone yell. "Jam your crank in his ass! That'll get him really bucking!" 5, 4, 3, 2, 1!

They all cheer as the stallion releases him, jumps off, and scatters away before the rhino has a chance for revenge yelling, "Gore! Gore! Gore!". "PAYBACK'S A BITCH!", the rhinos shouts in a weak attempt at a threat. He turns to his fellow rhinos and blurts out." Fuck you asshole!" as they all laugh at him.

The Rams, formed up in a ceremonial formation, start banging their shields and spears together. Awaiting the coming of the most revered figure they've grown to worship, Ares. They start chanting and hooting in anticipation. In unison and coordination, they begin a war dance ritual. Flailing their arms and stomping their feet. Pounding on their chests, then raising their spears in the air. Repeating until the anticipation is satisfied. Soon the first warrior Ram sees him and yells out, "FRONT AND CENTERED!". Slowly the others recognize their divinity. All together they bellow, "AAHHOOOAA! AAHHOOAA!". The platoon leader orders out, "RAM WARRIORS! FIGHTING STANCE! They all immediately close ranks with their shields up and spears poking through. "READY!" He bawls out. "Block, strike, block, strike, block, strike!" Without pause, the Rams raise their shields in, upper block, and thrust forward with their spears to display the accuracy and discipline of the skills they were instructed as a youth.

A young Stallion, seeing the performance, begins to laugh. Young stallion, "Look at those goofy Rams. Do you see this shit? They waste the sludging by repeating battle exercises, drills, and trying to impress their war-God. I should go over there and run right through the middle of them. Just to show how easy it is to break their ranks." Older Stallion replies, "Well you're right about one thing. It is a waste of sludge, but running through their ranks? Now that, I would never advise. Especially in the state that they're in. Those spears? Let's just say, it'll look like a family of porcupines tried crawling up your ass. And no-one here is going to go save you without meeting the same fate. But by all means, Go right ahead.".

Rhinos are looking onto the display the Rams are presenting. Thoroughly entertained by the scene they continue to watch until their visions can gain their attentions. Rhino 1 says, "Why can't we see Ares? I'm just saying. If he is real like they say he is. Why can't I experience or see what they do?" Rhino 2 educates, "Because you weren't meant to. Maybe I'm dead wrong on this, but your visions are customized to your own personal being. Based on your life experiences and what is meant for you to know and learn. You're a Rhino. Our visions tend to focus on a ancestor. Rams live their whole existence on Ares, so that's where their visions are themed.

While the Rams continue the courtship of their Ares, and Stallion making the most of their miscreant fun. The Weres and Terriers are fully invested in fighting with each. Testing each other's mettle and physical prowess. No-one wants to be viewed as the weakest of them, so everyone participates. Earning the respect of the strongest will be achieved no matter the outcome of the contest. Some may even be invited to join the Blood pack if they display exceptional perseverance and skills. It's an opportunity for those strong enough, or better yet brave enough, to challenge Roderick for a chance to lead. It is how he got his leadership position. The only time anyone dares to challenge is while under the influence of the sludge. The same holds true for the females of them. Rarely do the females challenge the males and only in one case did a female Werewolf lead the pack. A rising prospect throws down the challenge to Roderick by throwing a trench knife between his legs. His name is Convel.

Earned name from past battles. Meaning "wolf warrior". Ruby has been challenged by her equal. Bleyine, a female wolf looking to make a name for herself while taking her spot next to Roderick.

Roderick says to Convel," It is an honor. There is none other better I would expect to be confronted by. Sooner or later, I guess this day was bound to happen. If I go down today, there will be no shame in falling to you. Convel return with a passive aggressive insult," As I will feel no shame in replacing you.".

The two enter a makeshift arena outlined with huge rocks and surrounded by on lookers. Everyone has interest in the outcome.

All the commanders from each species are present. It didn't take long for individuals to choose sides and make side bets. Generally speaking, the younger of them rooted for Convel. The elders backed Roderick. The contest secures what everyone's agendas will be for the near future, as well as terminates any other challenger that may desire their position. A change of guard may influence the idea of new leadership amongst their kind. Roderick allows Convel to choose the level of force that is to be used in the challenge. Armed or unarmed. Traditionally the leader choses. Roderick is so well versed in any type of combat, that out of pure hubris, he allows Convel to decide. Convel declares unarmed combat, to the death, Roderick agrees. They begin circling each other randomly throwing out feeler strikes to size up each other. Convel jumps at Roderick with claws and fang extended. He attempted to make a quick dispatch of Roderick but as contact was made Roderick took his momentum and rolled backwards launching Convel into the cheering crowd. As Convel regains his composure, Roderick stood to his feet, turned, and faced his opponent. Convel acknowledged the quick counteraction with a nod. Convel re-thinks his approach and slowly, half steps toward Roderick, not to make the same mistake twice. Convel dove for Roderick's legs in hope of incapacitating him and ultimately take him to the ground. Roderick anticipated this maneuver and jumped through Canvel's arms, flipping around twisting on Convel's back, then landing to position himself for a rear naked blood choke. As Convel temporarily struggled to break himself free. He had to reason to Roderick's mercy by waving his hands in submission. Roderick had every right to end Convel's life but chose to release him. What would Roderick have to gain? The message to any other challengers was sent and understood.

Ruby, however, had to accept her opponent. Bleyine was a completely different ballgame. She wanted to fill the role as warrior queen. She wanted to earn the right to breed with the alpha male. She wanted to birth his children and supply the next generation of wolves. She trained, killed, and patiently waited for her opportunity to achieve her objective. As the two entered the arena Bleyine immediately attacked with little regard to strategy. Slightly off-guard Ruby stumbles back and regains her composure. Not knowing whether the details included weapons or not, she resorted back to basic instincts. Kill at all costs. Ruby pulls out a dagger from behind her back and begins to slash at Bleyine's neck. Bleyine realizes the severity of the situation stammering backwards and draws out her blade. With little regard for her own safety, Ruby charges forward and begins jabbing forward until eventually, one thrust sticks into Bleyine's chest. Ruby takes wounds, from Bleyine's weapon to her thigh before ultimately the velocity and aggression Ruby initiates, overpowers Bleyine as they both fall to the ground. As the battle finalizes Ruby keep stabbing Bleyine in her chest unnecessarily until there is no question who the victor was, and someone pulls her off. A Message was sent to any other challengers and vigorously received. Roderick and Ruby are undisputed leaders of the pack.

As other Weres and Terrier fight for their own positions in the pack, the Rhinos and Raptors have emersed themselves into their sludging. Strickland leads his birds of prey through a series of dives and tight maneuvering. Forcing themselves up in the air as high as possible, then rapidly diving, spinning in tight air circles all the way down until they were ground level before crashing. Low altitude flight weaving in between the rhinos. Dipping and dodging obstacles. Over and through the Ram's formation. Interrupting the fights happening in the arena by overwhelming the space with numbers so visibility is nonexistent. Loose, scattered feathers rain in the face of annoyed recipients. As the other species wildly make an attempt to catch a Rapture mid-flight, they turn it into a game. Few have the reaction reflexes to actually strike one down. The majority thankfully survive this ordeal.

The Rhinos finally have their sludge awakening realized. All their ancestors make their presence known, calling on the living to join them for counsel and recognition. The Rhinos separate in their owns spaces to receive their honored passing. Tank bows down to his father and father's father. They return his affections. He accepts counsel from them and their teachings. As the others get acquainted with their loved ones, all the other species leave them at peace. Allowing them their joy of reunion. Some see mothers. Other's siblings or past lovers. All agree, this wouldn't be the time to interrupt such a homecoming.

Aztec, being a novice to such experiences, is enduring a much different outcoming. He is reliving a recent drama that he experienced a short time ago. As the sludge maximizes its effects, he finds himself back during the time of the slaughtering of his family and sloths by the hands of Frank. He witnesses the reenactment of his sisters and brothers falling into a pit of stakes. His cubs being strangled to death with ropes by the primates. He watched hopelessly while sloths were gutted and skinned alive. Few were captured and taken away as prisoners. In Aztec's visions, he sees the joy and laughter of all the primates as they departed the crime scene. Leaving him and a handful of his warriors lying there to die. Fate would have it that such a fatality would not be.

Mud becomes extremely overjoyed. Dancing and singing songs of the Spider Streams.

Mud begins singing:

"I'm a bear of the spider Steams.
With barrels of honey, only hopes and dreams
I have no care at it would seem
We live the life of a king and queen."

Sherrian sees the nonsense in full swing. She shakes her head in disappointment. Knowing she won't be going anywhere anytime soon; she succumbs to her fate and grabs the serving giving to her. Mud sees his prospects come to pass. He Chants," Sher, Sher, Sher, Sher, Sher, Sher, Sher, Sher, Sher, Sher. She nods her head to Mud with disapproval. Giving up she says, "Fuck it!" then drinks. Mud cheers and claps in celebration. "There you go! Enjoy the ride!", he says. Sherrian throws the container, aiming for Mud's face and hitting him square between the eyes. "OH! Nice shot!", replies Mud, while he is rubbing his forehead. She lies back waiting for the personized prescience to take effect. Sherrian encounters a lone owl. A shadowy figure with green florescent eyes. Without movement from its mouth. Communication is clear. Messages to her are not ambiguous. Make peace with your past or suffer the same fate by the hands of others.

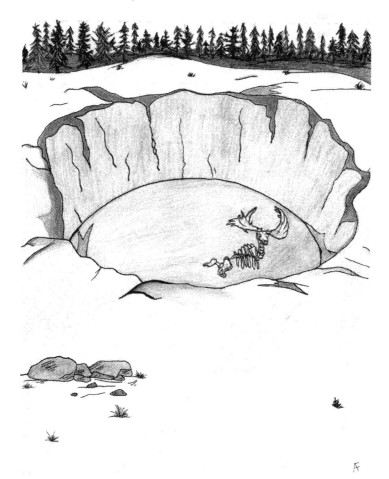

These same words kept being repeated over and over again by different species. An Owl initially, then repeated by a Terrier with green eyes. And a Ram, a Rhino, an Eagle, a lion, a Bengal, a Vampire, then lastly her Spider Stream cubs. Lost to a fight long forgotten. They all disappear. Her mother immerges and speaks, "Come sit with me my child. I understand your conflicts. There is a duality you will have to face. The decision will be a difficult one. I urge you to look to the light. There you will see the path you must take. You cannot be neutral. Live standing or die kneeling. These are your only choices. But you will live.". Sherrian is confused, "I don't understand.". Sherrian's mother replies, "You will. Be brave.". Just as fast as her mother appeared. Even quicker she leaves. She sees the face of Mud looking down on her. There is a short pause before Mud continues to sing in the background,

"I'm a bear of the spider Steams.
With barrels of honey, only hopes and dreams
I have no care at it would seem
We live the life of a king and queen."

She hesitantly joins in singing with him.

"I'm a bear of the spider Steams.
With barrels of honey, only hopes and dreams
I have no care at it would seem
We live the life of a king and queen."

12

ATTACK ON ALL FRONTS

ALL THE MAJOR AND LESSOR FAMILIES GATHER TO HEAR GOBLES, at his request. He reorganizes his thoughts to influence a guilty outcome. All of them have reservations of what is really happening. A coup d'état. They see nothing wrong with what Gobles has done, after given the rumors and hearing facts. As far as they are concerned, Goble's actions are consistent with what other leaders have done in the past. Any action against the Weres are encouraged. Out of respect they will entertain what Henrick has to say. Clearly, they are becoming increasingly impatient with what has transpired. Goble begins," Esteemed aristocrats. We have gathered here to examine whether our laws and traditions and been violated. Clearly, they have, based on current attestation. I now ask you. Need we expire more time asking questions to gather more points of evidence? Will we be forced to continue such a charade, when it is obviously known that Gobles, should be removed from power and sent to the afterlife. Alarick Bornbrick directs his words to the accuser, "Henrick, I speak to you with the utmost acclaim. You, your family, have earned your standing and position amongst the Vampire Nation. However! Although you make points beyond dispute, Our Family is willing to overlook the technicality you bring attention to. Based on previous conflicts with the Weres, or any other circumstances that may have risen.". Quite frankly Henrick, this is a waste of our time. There are much more pressing issues needing attending to. You should see to it that they are given the proper and immediate attention warranted.". Henrick replies, "This is dispiriting to say the least. I underestimated the resolve of our coterie.".

As Henrick called for the examination to resume, there is a commotion of warfare felt from outside the ruins. They all make their way to the closest porthole to witness what seems to be an attack on the Plexidus and Plexidor convoy. Stakes airborne through the mist aiming directly into their escorting guards. As warriors scramble to take cover and regroup for a counterattack, the members of both families retreat toward the ruins as the sun rises. The worst time for the Vamps to be under attack. The solar burn doesn't kill them alone but does severely weaken them. Each member is randomly killed off by the arial projectiles. As the other families look on, Droskon Voldimote looks to Hendrick and demands he issues orders to assist. Henrick resists, "They must be sacrificed for our safety. We cannot open the gates and allow further vulnerability. The sun has risen. We cannot risk the masses for the few.". Alearick Bornbrick demands," FREE GOBLE AND THE 100 FEW YOU ARRESTED! ALLOW THEM TO REPELL THESE TRANGRESSORS!". Henrick continues his reasoning, "That is not an option. He is likely to kill us as much as he is those who would have the impudence to attack our bureau.". Droskon Voldimot blurts out, "You are derelict in you sworn duties! This will follow you closely and far into the future!".

The onslaught continues. The silver coated projectiles meet their intended mark as both families beg for assistance. The Plexidus and Plexidor's family security ready themselves for a counterattack. They all footslog forward toward the oncoming assault. As they slowly trudge closer being picked off one at a time. Out of a tree line rushes a closely formed elephant herd. Tusked extended coated with silver. Rushing forward, the helpless few are left to their demise, brace themselves for an inevitable impact. The herd skew, trample and make waste to everything in their path. It just was a matter of time before the leftovers were dispatched of their lives. The onlookers are horrified. Shortly after an army gathers outside the ruins. Made up of Frank's commanders and their soldiers. Equipped with demolition apparatuses. Trebuchets, catapults, and ballistae. Droskon turns to Henrick, "This cannot continue. If you will do nothing Henrick, I will take action.". Henrick responds with violence. He draws a silver blade and plants it into Droskon's heart with no hesitation ending his life. He raises his weapon to the others, points and says," We will stand fast! I am the last word!".

Crashing against the stonewall the assault continues. The main egress has been breached. Pouring through, armed mutated Hippo/Human hybrids make their intentions known. They were met with little resistance by young Vamps unable to match the strength of their advance. Outside the ruins, warrior primates surround the compound in attempt to secure anyone who tempts to escape. While heavy Hippo infantry funnel in to help clear anyone looking to repel, light infantry primate foot soldiers follow behind and attack weakened vampires to their own peril. The mass numbers allow every inch of the Vampire ruins to be consumed. Defenders of all the families are slayed as the head of each monarch begins to panic. From a distance Thanani and her force draw close to the ruins and hear a familiar sound. Battle formations and clashes. She rushes from a covered forest-line undetected and assesses the situation. Cajole exclaims, "That's him! That is Frank's forces. But I don't see him.". Thanani replies," It appears an intervention is in order.". She calls for Kodi and Azizi to ready their soldiers. She quickly devises a plan. "The Bears will lead the charge to break through their weakest line. Followed by Azizi and half his forces. Their task is to press through to the inside of the ruins. Then seek and destroy anything that moves. The other half of Azizi's warriors will follow me, Gur, Thorn, and Bandit's forces. First attacking the light infantry ground forces, then anyone else left standing. Any questions?". Adrina quickly adds, "There is an underground tunnel not far from here. It leads to the dungeons under the ruins. If my calculations are correct, Gobles is there and most likely his chosen one hundred held in examination cells. Shall I seek to free Gobles and his elite?". Thanani agrees, "Yes. And take Cajole with you. Cajole eagerly says, "Adrina, let's get moving. We're running out of time". Frank's forces press forward through every hallway and room they encounter. No space is left unmolested. The wave of onslaught appears to be unstoppable until they arrive at a reenforced stone door. Demolition, battering rams, and other useful siege equipment are brought to the forefront. As the inevitable breech into the room continues, panic sets in on the other side. Alearick pleas for action, "What are we going to do Henrick? Is this your plan? We sit here and wait to be slaughtered? This is a disaster!".

Henrick looks around frantically trying to find a way out. Any choice they make leads to certain death. He orders everyone to arm themselves and prepare to fight. With little weapons to utilize, armor to protect themselves, and tactical knowledge in warfare, they form a pathetic wall to repel the enemy. In quick time the last line of defense is brought down. The defenders make a weak attempt to hold back those who enter but inevitably begin to fail. As the final few vampires left standing ready themselves to die. A distraction gains the attention of the attackers. Azizi and his hyenas engage the rear guard. They penetrate through into the room and engage a vicious attack on Frank's final few left. Cajole and Adrina make it to the holding cells where Gobles and is loyal warriors are kept. They successfully release them of their confines, then lead them back out. They witness the retreat of all Frank's sieging warriors as Thanani finishes off the last of those ignorant enough to challenge her. In their weakened state, they avoid any confrontation with those looking for a last fight.

At the Grand Owl's home range, an army of Blakiston's Fish owls are strategically posted surrounding the grove headquarters. Camouflaged into the tree line, they are alert and aware of the approaching threat. From a far distance to anyone other than owls, it looks like a swarm of locusts. The distance that these aggressors need to travel, gives an early warning system. They have less than a minute before they are completely engulfed. The alarm is sounded. Owls appear almost out of nowhere. Most spearhead courageously toward the incoming fight. A second defense wave of owls takes its position guarding what best they can in front of larger entry points. Within seconds of sighting the intruders, a midair fight begins. Talons extended, the owls will soon discover these raptors are much smaller and much more difficult to handle. Hummingbirds hybrids. The owls hopelessly capture and quickly kill as many as they can catch. They moment they take precious time to kill one, many more fly by unrelenting. It would be minutes after the first contact that they reach the tree line of the grove. Another desperate attempt to repel the invaders begin. The home range will soon be overwhelmed with small raptors. The owls quickly realize that these small birds have one purpose. To fill in all the dead space for the real assault. A loud screech is heard in the distance. The owls who are out in the open, pause. Then they understand the true danger they're in. Wingspan in sizes never seen before. Twice the length of their own. Condors and vultures swooping down upon them. As the hummingbirds were to the owls, so are the owls to these raptors. The real fight for life begins. The owls in the first wave are decimated in short order. Massive talons from these colossal, flying birds of prey are directed at the grove. The Grand Owl is well aware of the dangerous position he's in. He readies himself in the ways he knows how for a retreat. Centurion warns," Sir, we need to leave now! There is no time to wait. We are being overwhelmed. Sir!" Grand Owl replies, "I'm ready, let's go.". Trying to make their leave, their presence is alerted by birds coating the branches of the escape route. An escort of bodyguards do their best to silence the sound. It's futile. Too many to kill, too hard to catch. Retreating is priority. The end of the escape route is soon to be encountered, but before it could be achieved, It's blocked by several Andean condors. A vicious, blood lust battle begins. The Owls are much more maneuverable in flight and can confuse and overwhelm their counterparts. This doesn't last long however, as hawks enter the fray. Assisting in a fight against the owls, these hawks mount an unrelenting attack that dramatically turns the tide in their favor. The Grand Owl makes a last desperate attempt at escaping by diving and spinning away from those who would have him in their talons. Narrowly dodging one after the next Condor at the sacrifice of his protectors who place themselves in between danger and freedom, Boris sees open skies but is snatched out of the air by a Condor and taken down. As the last of the Owls escape or are killed off. An imposing figure to Boris appears to him.

Frank meets Boris for the first time, "So, this is the 'Grand Owl' I hear so much about. I expected something a little more, impressive.". Boris replies, "As Did I.". Frank amused," HAHAHAH! That is a good one. I can appreciate a snappy comeback. The thing is. I have met all types of fun and exciting creatures. I've had my fair share of witty mind battles. A kind of, shall I say, intellectual chess. In the end it wasn't my mind that won. It was the business end of my sharpened sword. And you, my feathered friend, are at of a great disadvantage.". Boris says, "Look behind you.". Frank turns to look over his shoulder and is startled by a strike force of swarming raptors of all kinds led by Quaid. Knocking Frank over, he loses his sword. The birds of prey claw at Frank and all his forces causing enough mayhem to free Boris. This small attack contingency gives Quaid and Boris enough time to retreat into safety. Frank and his warrior regain the upper hand but are unable to make sense of what has just happened before they realize Boris has escaped. Disappointed, Frank says sarcastically to his subordinates, "Well. Did no-one see that coming.? Not one of you could have said, Hey boss there's an incoming flock of attacking birds. I had to hear it from THE

FUCKING OWL THAT WAS FUCKING CAPTURED!". None
speak. "No? That's unfortunate."

Back at the Wolf's refuge everyone who partook in the
sludging is either still intoxicated, recovering with a hangover,
or sleeping off the effects. There are very few left to protect the
others and even less, fully capable of defending off an attack. Mud
lays snoring happily in the pit next to Sherrian. Aztec, having
consumed more than necessary, still sufferings from the visions
of his people being slaughtered. He randomly and wildly fights off
the battles in his mind. Roderick, Ruby and all his commanders
have recovered and are gathered to give a status on their soldier's
fighting status. All are in attendance except Bronze, who is still in
his orgasmic state, looking for those willing to mate. Baxter says,
"My Rams, whether inebriated or not, are motivated and ready
for battle.". Tank reports, "We'll need some time. A day perhaps.".
Strickland gives his status, "We're ineffective right now. Still need
some time.". Muscles adds "I'll say half my terriers are ready.".
Ruby finishes, "Weres all good.". Pointing to the horses Roderick
notes, "And the fucking stallions are still enjoying their sludge. We
have a huge decision to make. If what Quaid says is true. And I
for one, believe him. Then that means we must find a way, for the
time being, to make peace and join forces with Thanani. Or face
complete annihilation up against this Frank.". Tank asks, "But will
she fight side by side with us?". Baxter asks, "Can her forces hold
up their end of the fight if they do?". Ruby reminds them, "If they
agree to fight alongside us, we all know she, and those who fight
alongside her, are more than capable of holding up their end.".
Strickland continues the discussion, "We all know this firsthand.
The real question is. Will the VN?". Roderick gives his thoughts,
"My guess is the VN is not much of a threat without her. Look at
past battles. Have they ever fought without the help of anyone?".
Bronze breaks up the seriousness, "Hey everyone! Anyone want
to... Yaa know?". Tank annoyed scolds him," Go find someone

and somewhere else to fuck!", Bronze gleefully responds," Ok! You're missing out!". Baxter, amazed adds, "SERIOUSLY?". Suddenly, a horn sounds the alarm. Bodies start scrambling about. Everyone stands up to look in the direction of the warning. An Eagle flies and lands in the middle of the huddle to brief everyone on an impending fight.

Centurion reports, "Gentlemen, Ruby. A mile out, there is a fully equipped army approaching. They appear to be in battle formation, armed, and beating war drums. And sir. They have elephants.".

Roderick gathers all his able-bodied warrior. The Rams, still feeling the effects of the sludging, not completely recovered, form the frontline wall. The rhinos are still fast asleep, and no one is able to wake them from their trance. The Stallions are basically useless but those that can fight, line up on either end of the rams. Some Weres mount the back of the Broncos and the Terriers position themselves behind the Rams. Other smaller, lighter Terriers mount the bigger Rams. The Eagles take to flight. Some carry large boulders, while others load their bows into the strings of their arrows. They Hover hundreds of feet in the air, ready to unleash death from above. Mud, Sherrian, and Aztec, slightly in their delusional state, are alerted to the current events. Mud speaks," Something is happening. The war horn has sounded.". Hopeful Sherrian replies, "Wonder if it's Thanani.". Mud says, "Possibly. Let's go see. I left us a way out.". They all make their way up and out of the pit. Sherrian mentions, "Finally, I can go home.". Aztec, blood thirsty and delusional, makes his intentions known, "I'll KILL YOU ALL YOU MOTHER FUCKERS!". From a distance they can hear the trumpets from a dozen elephants. Light vibrations are felt in the ground, steadily getting stronger. Mud makes his way to the frontline next to Ruby. He turns around and sees Sherrian leaving the battlefield. He thinks to himself, *"Don't leave."* Emotionally defeated, he turns back focusing on his commitment. He can hear from behind Aztec struggling with his sludging. Wildly swinging, attempting to kill his visions. Mud thinks, *"This is what Quaid must have been talking about."*. Ruby speaks under her breath, "This is a problem.". Roderick unleashes his instructions," NO QUARTERS GIVEN! KILL ANYTHING THAT ISN'T US!". Everyone Screeches out a war cry. From behind the elephants appear black rhinos charging alongside. A surprising familiar agitator emerges. KOMODOS! The Komodo Dragons have been addicted to revenge after Roderick and his army all but killed off their kind. Riding on the top of the Elephants and Rhinos are countless primates of all kinds. They listen to the primate's hoots, grunts, and barks as a clash of two opposing forces collide. Strickland activates the order to the very few raptors that are capable of engaging. A rain of boulders and arrows rain down on the charge. Some missing their targets, others bouncing off the mammoths like an annoying flea causing no damage. But an acceptable amount due cause significant damage to the primates, knocking them off their seated position and ending their battle campaign. The charge continues. Roderick orders forward and warns of being trampled. The two sides finally collide. Mud claws, bites, and maws any primate willing to engage. He quickly becomes overwhelmed by numbers. As he is going down, he senses a familiar presence. Sherrian and a mind bent Aztec. They rip, and tear at those that would see Mud bloodied and dead. He regains his fighting position and takes his place with his back to his saviors. The Rams, in their stubborn bravery, smash head on with the Rhinos and Elephants, only to be nearly trampled. The Terriers, Weres and Raptors engage the Komodo and primates, killing everything that moves. In a twisted, humorous turn of events, many stallions still intoxicated, enter the fray, only to hold down their victims and literally fuck them to death. At least the smaller bodied warriors. Drastically outnumbered and undersized. Roderick's Army is losing the battle with half his forces on the sidelines and the Rhinos unable to assist. Strickland gains Roderick attention, "Something else is approaching from the rear.". Roderick replies, "Who or what is it? Can you tell?". Strickland reports bad news, "LIONS AND HYENAS! IT'S THANANI!". Ruby senses a pending doom, "FUCK! WHAT IS SHE DOING?". The Eagles watch closely from above. Some leave and gather more ammunition to unload from sky. They witness what is the beginning of what the past would describe as impossible. Thanani spreads her forces across the battlefield. Charging in a unified straight line, with the cheetahs on each side and bigger cats centered, Gur is leading the charge. Thorn, Azizi with his hyenas, and wild dogs closely behind, with bears flanking them.

Racoon hybrids follow the lead at a distance to kill any leftovers. Closing in fast at breakneck speed, Roderick says in a low tone. Roderick thinks to himself, *This is about to get interesting.*".

13

UNITED BY LOSS

IN QUICK TIME GUR MAKES FIRST CONTACT. IN A BLINDING RAGE, he dispatches several Komodo and primates before anyone else makes contact. Thanani shouts out. "ATTACK THE ELEPHANT'S EYES!" Her orders are repeated throughout the ranks. Upon hearing the chatter, soon Roderick relays the same orders. The Raptors dive forward toward the Elephants. Terriers, Bears, Grims, Hyenas along with the wild dogs, Rams, and Raccoons use any means necessary to first, attack the elephants' eyes. Blinded and unable to effectively fend off an attack. The Elephants are consumed with death. With the behemoths off the killing field, the last of Frank's forces are decimated. A small contingency of dying rhinos retreat. Thanani and Roderick's armies face off on opposite sides. Warriors still capable of fighting, gather for protection with their weapons pointed at their opposition. Both side growl, yell, hiss, threaten, display their own signs of aggression, but never make the first move to engage each other physically. Roderick calls for Ruby with no response. Keeping his eye on Thanani again he repeats for Ruby to join him with no response. "RUBY!", he shouts. Fear sets in. He begins to panic, unable to address both Thanani as a threat, and his missing love. The cry for her whereabouts breaks the focus everyone has on each other. Thanani lowers her knife. Keeping one eye on Roderick, she issues orders out to her comrades, "STAND DOWN! Assist in finding Ruby. When you find her, she is not to be touched. You will alert Roderick of her position and protect her with your life.".", Looking at Roderick she adds, "If need be."

A massive search party is sent out on both sides. Roderick and his commanders sit quietly facing Thanani and her warriors. A sister lion of Sheeba returns and whispers into Thanani's ear. Roderick stands and readies himself to hear feedback. She orders that all her subordinates arm themselves and form up in a guarded posture. Uneasy, she faces Roderick as Gur and Thorn take position next to her on guard. The blood pack, Muscles, Baxter, and Strickland do the same for Roderick. Thanani speaks, "They've found Ruby. They are bringing her to you as we speak. She's alive. Barely.". Fear and anger take over Roderick. Adrenaline rushes through everyone. Tensions are extremely high. The worst-case scenario starts to sink into onlooker's psyche. A part in the crowd slowly opens up and is seen from a distance. As a procession pushes through, warriors take their battle gear off and bow their heads. Roderick shoves bodies out of his way to rush forward through the crowd. His fears are met with reality. The lioness' lay Ruby's body at his feet. He grabs her in caress. She opens her weary eyes to see her wolf's face. Ruby apologizes," I'm sorry." She lies with little strength taking short, rapid breaths finding it difficult to breath, she makes every attempt to inhale, but a puncture womb to her lungs leaves her struggling for her life. Roderick weeps and listens to her final words, "I will soon see the shits that did this to me again. I won't let this happen to me in the afterlife.". Roderick pulls her into him tightly embracing his chest to hers. He whispers to her, "I'm sorry, It's ok. Rest. I'll see you soon.".

She closes her eyes one last time, and her body goes limp. Roderick looks up at Thanani and her guardians. With tears in his eyes, he stands ups, unsheathes his sword, and points it at Thanani. With hand and sword trembling, he lets out a painful raging war scream. Gur carefully walks over to Roderick's trembling body and grips the sharpened blade. He stares at Roderick who is looking through him. Blood droplets drip off Gur's hand. He assists in lowering his blade. Drawing Roderick close to him in a brotherly hug. He attempts to comfort Roderick knowing he'll fail. Gur tells him, "We Understand. We know your pain. Together. REVENGE!". Muscles walks over and hands Roderick a lock of Ruby's hair. He touches him on the shoulder and says, "For Ruby.". Strickland, Tank, Baxter, Bronze, Mud, and all their warriors present, follow suit, offering the same gesture of respect. In solidarity and in unison. Thanani, Kodi, Thorn, Bandit, and all who fight for her begin chanting, RUBY! RUBY! RUBY! This initiates everyone to join in.

All rituals, rites and observances were given in preparation and execution for Ruby's final good-byes. Each side separates themselves to their selected grounds as Roderick and Thanani sit at a huge bonfire. Representatives include Roderick, Muscles, Baxter, Strickland, Tank, Bronze, and Mud. Opposite to them is: Thanani, Gur, Azizi, Thorn, Bandit, Kodi, and Hecate. Hecate has been offered a position of leadership for his devotion and fighting skills leading his cheetahs. Tensions continue to be extremely high. It won't take much to spark an all-out battle. Everyone is looking to justify the first move. No-one knows how to open the floor for dialogue. All know it needs to commence somehow by someone. Bronze decides he will take on the challenge.

He attempts to break the anxiety with horse humor, "My stallions are completely spent from fucking.". None laugh. Tank responds with distain," Really? This is what we're doing now?". "Honestly!", Baxter seconds. Bronze replies, "Well, I don't hear you two saying anything of worth!". Gur takes this jawing back and forth, as an opportunity to help break the ice. "Roderick, I'm sure you might be wondering where Sheeba is.". Roderick doesn't respond. Gur continues, "When we left the battlefield against your forces, it was on the intel that a primate, who stands for nothing but death, has declared war on us. The VN, the owls, and anyone who stands in his way. That includes you. You Baxter, you Bronze, you Tank, you Strickland, you Muscles, and yes you too Mud. We hesitated, but convincing reason forced us to investigate. As you saw, abandoning the battlefield as we did, only to go back to the VN ruins and encounter the same forces we just fought off here today. I understand that every warrior is a loss but none dearer to me, as Ruby was to you, Roderick. I lost my lioness from the tusk of elephant through her chest. She threw herself in front of that elephant protecting me. Just as she has always done in the past. More times than I have done for her.". Upon hearing about Sheeba, Roderick looks to his most trusted and says, "We will honor her sacrifice in the way she deserves.". Understanding the love between life partners, Thanani offers her condolences," My heart bleeds for both of your losses. We empathize with the pain of our friends, and foes. It is most felt when we women self-sacrifice for our male counterparts. This Frank has taken Sheeba from our world, and now Ruby from yours. The only question needing to be addressed now is, What's next? Are we going to do what we all know must be done? Don't mistake me, we have the same animosity toward all of you, as you do towards us. We will never forget what led to this point, and we don't expect you all to either. Here's the thing. This fighting, this war, may in fact resume at some point. Now, later, or never. But as apprehensive as we all are sitting right here, we must join forces and address this new threat. You all know this we must do.".

"And what of the Vampire Nation?", Roderick asks. He adds, "What we all know to be a fact is, they care nothing but themselves. They are an odious and execrable institution. What will be their stance?". Gur answers, "Gobles has pledged his vampires to this cause. We all here, do not completely trust him, as we assume you never will. However, he and his people have lost as much as we have. They have much to benefit by making peace and joining forces as any of us. We are confident he and his vampires will do their part. Afterwards, we cannot vouch for.". Muscles asks, "So where is Gobles? Why is he not here expressing this alongside you?". Azizi announces, "He is getting his Vampire Nation in order.".

Outside The Vampire Nation ruins, Gobles has turned the grounds into an execution, death encampment. With his most loyal, battle tested commanders overseeing the coming events, Goble purposefully segregated two special execution crucifixes that centers them all. Elevated for all to see. One for Henrick, who Gobles sees as the instigator and lead mutineer. And a second cross, facing the first, for the Emissary who arrested Gobles on the battlefield. Surrounding the two, are a series of guillotines and wooden posts meant for restraining and staking the guilty. All will be in attendance to watch the spectacle. It is meant as a warning to would be transgressors attempting to unseat future authorities, as well as eliminate rivals. Gobles, feeling a bit full of himself, walks over to where Henrick and his emissary accomplice are apprehended; tied up and secured with ropes that have threads of silver woven inside. Adrina sits on his shoulder. Cajole walks over taking in what he sees and stands next to him. Goble proudly observes his glory and says, "Well, isn't this a strange turn of events. Adrina replies, "Strange indeed.". Emissary begins to plead with Gobles, "I was following my orders. The law is clear. I have done nothing to justify this execution.". Adrina giggles and mentions to Gobles, "Following his orders he says.". Goble answers the emissary's comments, "Maybe you're right. Maybe, you did carry out your orders in accordance with the law. But see I don't like you. Your pale skin and disrespectful smirk offended me. I can't seem to forget how impudent you were not too long ago. But the satisfaction of watching you burn into dust soon will help. Won't it Adrina?". Adrina agrees, "It'll help indeed, sire. He did try to eat me, so you know.". Goble replies, "That is unfortunately." Looking at the emissary he continues, "And your son. He will forever be on the frontline of every battle, conflict, and shit job, I see fit for a thousand years. But you Henrick. Your sons and daughters, hell, your whole legacy will die with you here today. We can't have an oath of vengeance because of your staking tonight. Adrina adds, "Can't have that! Now that. Would. Not. Be. Good.". Cajole tries to get things sped up, "Sire, can we get on with this? We have a lot to prepare for these next coming days.". Gobles remarks, "See that Henrick? Cajole is so blood thirsty right now. He's so impatient. Very well. On with it then.". Gobles slowly walks up on a stage build for the event and turns to address all that have been forced to witness the deaths of the traitors. Dark ink bleeds out of his eyes from his anger. He pauses and gathers his thoughts, not realizing drool seeping out from between his sharped extended teeth. He turns around to face his subjects. With subdued aggression and vengeance in his voice, Gobles takes a deep breath to spew his soliloquy. "My fellow citizens of the Vampire Nation. Tonight, is a sad, sad evening. You have been called to these sacred grounds to bear witness to justice being enacted. These Vampires you see before you have been accused and convicted of crimes against our nation. They include mutiny, conspiracy, treason, Theft by Deception, and Aiding the Enemy. Henrick and his rogue vampires conducted an illegal examination, in an attempt to overthrow our system of government and seize power for himself. He arrested and incarcerated our most elite warriors unlawfully. Your brothers and sisters! Your most beloved and honored soldiers.

While our warriors were illegally confined, this left our Ruins unprotected and venerable to attack. His actions subsequently became the enemy's greatest weapon in their attack. This is justification for execution here today. Let this be a dire warning to those that seek to commit these same crimes. Know that this will be your fate as well.". Adrina repeats, "Your fate as well.". Goble snaps is fingers and immediately vampires walk over to their respective convicted vampires with a stake. As vampires receive their final sentencing with sharpened pieces of wood pressed into their hearts. Sounds of hissing, crying out from family members, and cheers of joy from those approving is heard. They leave Henrick and his Emissary for last. Goble walks over to the emissary and reminds him of his disrespect before he plunges a stake in his heart. He turns around to face Henrick. Henrick struggles and hisses, anticipating the outcome. Gobles wastes no time is punching a hole through Henrick's bare chest and ripping out his rotting heart. Before Henrick takes his final breath, Goble shoves and grinds it into Henrick's open mouth. Gobles turns to address the onlookers, "As distasteful as that episode was to endure, we look to a new day. A new start. The beginning of an era commences. The age of Vampire rule. We begin with the complete annihilation of this Frank and his minions. It ends with Thanani, Roderick and the lot of them! ".WHOLE LOT OF THEM!", Adrina emphasizes. Cajole looks on in the background with concern. Understanding the coming event will be challenging.

Quad and Boris make their way toward the Werewolf refuge with an Army of guardians and centurions. Stopping only to hydrate at a random lake and quickly rest. Along the way Boris says nothing. Quaid fires off question after question. Who, what, when, where, and how? Still Boris says nothing. Focused on making it to his destination and the next steps. Finally, the uncomfortable silence is broken when Boris acknowledges his mistake, Boris, "I'm sorry. I made a mistake.". Quaid replies, "Don't feel obligated to apologize to me. I wasn't looking for one.". Boris corrects him, "I wasn't. I was apologizing to my ancestors, my teachers, and most important, to myself. I don't owe you, nor anyone else my regrets.". Quaid says, "I didn't mean to…". Boris interrupts, "I did what it was meant for me to do. I will continue to do that. Once we get to the refuge, I will help devise a plan with Roderick and Thanani. Giving any assistance within my abilities and contacts. The Vampire Nation is on their way to the refuge.". Quaid excited says, "So, they did join forces! This is great news.". Boris cautions, "Maybe, maybe not. This union is unprecedented. At least as far as my memory goes back. This could be a most powerful alliance. Or it may be the death of us all. Time will only tell. One thing I know for sure. These are uneasy times. None are safe. Tragedy has already come to the forefront.". Boris, Quaid, and their escorts finally make it to the refuge. They are greeted by all with embracing brotherhood and admiration. Many appear to be deflated by his appearance understanding what it means. Others curious. Boris makes himself comfortable with the other faction leaders while Quaid goes to find Azizi. Boris updates everyone on the recent tribulations. Those listening to Boris are satisfied that everything everyone testified to, is confirmed to be true. They all know without doubt that they must unite. The easy part has concluded. The hard part is not just convincing their warriors but ensuring that they fight as a single unit. Sacrificing for one another, if need be, for a recent common enemy. How will they be able to build trust and camaraderie amongst all grudges not yet healed? Who has seniority? Who makes the final decisions on what or any matters? For hours suggestions and ideas are brought to the table. Many are discarded as unrealistic. Few accepted. They all agree that they all must train together. Intertwined. Their warriors must be put into situations where their cooperation is needed and sacrifice for one another is put to the test. They arrive at a final intent.

Boris speaks," So, it is agreed upon. I want to thank all the commanders here for you vote of confidence. As a neutral party, I will do my best to be fair, firm, and consistence. Taking into consideration the consequences of my choices. To show my sincerity, I will enact AUX ARMES. A call to arms of my kind and all who follow me. They will be attached to Strickland's command. I assure you Strickland, they will follow your orders.". Strickland replies, "as you say". Boris continues, "We will break up each unit by species from Roderick's champions, and pair them with the champions from Thanani's army. They will go on a hunting expedition for prey to feed their respective sides. They will need to work together if they are to be successful because they will be competing against the other hunting parties. Roderick and Thanani. Pair your warriors up. Roderick orders," Muscles step forward.". Thanani counters, "Azizi step forward.". Muscles grins as Azizi gets within inches of his nose. The largest of the selected Terriers gets in between them focused and staring into the eyes of Azizi. Azizi extends his forearm and hand in an attempt to show his cooperation and truce. After an uncomfortable short pause, Muscles gentle moves his bodyguard aside and returns the gesture by receiving Azizi's extended hand. The others follow their leader's suit by embracing their mirrored comrades.

Thanani orders the next to step up, "Bandit step forward.". Roderick says, "Strickland step forward.". Strickland takes to flight followed by those he would lead. Climbing heights of over a thousand feet. They nosedive directly toward Bandit and his Raccoons. Reaching maximum speeds well over one hundred miles per hour, all are unsure of the outcome or how to respond. Before making contact, they change their flight pattern into a circular motion flying around those massed at ground zero. The sheer speed causes a strong wind force powerful enough to blind those not smart enough to protect their eyes from the dirt being kicked up. They finally land in front of the chosen Raccoons. "Bravo", whispers Bandit while clapping and nodding his head in approval.

Roderick calls the next commander, "Bronze step forward.". Then Thanani "Hecate step forward.". Hecate steps in front of Bronze sizing him up. Bronze challenges, "Word is here you cats are pretty fast.". Hecate proudly replies, "Faster than your stallions, that I know for sure." Bronze counters, "Maybe at first, but for how long. Do you cats have the stamina to keep pace I wonder?". "You'd be surprised.". Hecate says.". Bronze tries to shut him up, "We'll assess you speed.". "As we will your stamina.",

Hecate threatens. They both smile looking each other up, then return to their respective sides.

Thanani calls for Kodi and Sherrian to step forward. Roderick, Tank and Mud filled with excitement says to Sherrian, "Hi love! We're going to be hunting together!". Sherrian shouts, "Shut up!". Kodi talks first, "So, Tank, is it? Do you any clever words for me? Perhaps some display of strength or speed? Tank looks at his new hunting companions unimpressed and replies, "I'm quite sure you're already well aware of our talents. And I'm not much of a talker so spare me. I have had my fill of prattle from the horses.". Both sides take position mixing in with each other quietly. Roderick calls the next half of those teaming up, "Bloodpack and Aztec step forward.". Thanani equals his challenge, "Gur, and Thorn, and the sisters of Sheeba. Step forward.".

The intensity goes from zero to a hundred in the blink of an eye. The Blood pack begins violently barking and kicking up dirt with their hind legs in the direction of the cats. Foam spraying out of their mouths making a mess of the scene. Aztec's hair raises on his back unsure of what is happening. He threatens with his own saw warning in all direction toward anyone that may have ill intent toward him. In return the sisters of Sheeba roar and crouch down in a show of power and strength in response. Both sides try to intimidate the other in their own display of intensity and aggression. Neither side coming in contact with the other, knowing that it would have crossed the line and broken the truce. Gur and Thorn looking at the scene amused. In unison, they quiet everyone with a trembling roar. Shaking the insides of all in attendance. Silence takes over and everyone stares at the two impressed yet intimidated at the same time. Roderick calls for the last of his leaders, "Baxter step forward.". Baxter looks around wondering who he and his rams will have to tolerate. Speaking to Thanani he says, "And who will pair with us?". Gobles answers from a distance," My best vampires will take up the challenge.".

Adrina repeats," His vampires!'". Gobles continues," We know of your agreement already. On behalf of the VN. We accept your negotiations.". Cajole interjects, "I have called my Fox skulk to answer the bid to combat. They will answer. I would have them pair with the Wolves.". Roderick nods his head in agreement. All others see no disagreement in Cajole's logic. Boris finalizes the negotiations, "So shall this union be sealed. All champions, familiarize yourselves with your new brothers and sisters. You leave here broken, unsure. You return as one. Return here with the past forgotten, and the future hopeful. You all leave at the break of sunlight.". Thanani, Roderick, Gur, Thorn, Boris, Gobles, Adrina and Cajole sit in a circle discussing the future possibilities. Roderick feeling vulnerable being the only representative from his army, but also empowered by his show of courage, knowing he is surrounded by those that would have killed him a short time ago. He is comforted in knowing his allies would avenge him if any betrayal were suspected. Goble makes an observation, "Well, who would have guessed this a year ago?". Adrina, "Year ago!". Boris answers confidently, "The Sloths.". Cajole adds, "This is an outlandish and unlikely alliance.". Thorn asks, "What to do now?". Roderick suggests,". We hunt.". Gur, confirming the same thoughts is with him, "We hunt.".

14

THE RESPONSE

FRANK GATHERS UP ALL HIS COMMANDERS. HE SITS ON TOP OF his favorite pachyderm, Matilda. After years of battle, she has turned into a deadly war elephant. She obeys and fights, not out of love for Frank, honor, or any code. Not for praises of grandeur about being a great mystical warrior. Her reasoning is simple, yet the most powerful reason of all to fight. Her young ones are being held as hostages. Their lives depend on her obedience to kill. Her willingness to live. Her death seals the fate of theirs. All her fellow mammoths fight under these grave conditions. Frank orders only the immediate subordinates under his command to appear in attendance to bear witness, but even the lesser fighters who aren't there have an understanding of what is about to happen. His subdued wrath begins," Ladies and gentlemen, what just happened here? Why am I standing here with my thumb up my ass wondering why the results I anticipated, never came to fruition? I mean, you all did have every advantage a commander could ask for. Especially in numbers. Did you not outnumber these wretched creatures? You all even had the element of surprise. Everything was perfectly set up for success. But unfortunately, it was they, not we, who enacted the violence of action. Why? Why did we not anticipate the unanticipated? Why did we not think of every possible scenario with a plan of action to counter their counter? Why did those under your all command fear the enemy more than the idea of failing you? I blame myself. I blame myself because I failed you. I allowed you all to plan, arrange recon, make recon, complete the planning, issue all the orders, and supervise the battlefield. Somewhere deep down I knew you all were going to fail. Maybe I wanted you all to. Hm? Maybe. I'm so confused at this point. So many unanswered questions. Yet no-one has attempted to explain. Smart. Your answers will sound like excuses I will not accept. Still, will anyone please speak up and help me understand? It'll make me feel better.".

Frank jumps off Matilda to look his commanders in their eyes. He stands in front of his most senior advisor. He begins to adjust his commander's uniform, so his personal appearance is at an acceptable level to present himself.

Frank asks, "Commander Barcan, you have been on more campaigns than any other. No-one here is more senior to you, at least none here that I'm aware of has fought longer and harder for me. You are family by spiritual union. You have married my sister. My wife's sister, but none the less my sister. We are brothers. So, when I come to you and ask questions, I am confident that I will receive a true and honest answer. I know I will get the truth, won't I? Commander Barcan replies, "Yes, sir you will.". Frank continues, "Great! Please, In the most direct and forthright answer. Please tell me what happened?". Commander Barcan pauses to think and counter with an acceptable answer. Without hesitation Frank presents a sharpened eight-inch blade and thrusts into the neck of his commander silencing him forever. Barcan drops to his knees holding the projectile impaled into his neck. Unable to speak or breath he slowly dies quietly. Frank moves on, placing his hand on his next victims shoulder he begins to fix his uniform. He tells him, "And you. You will marry my poor widowed sister. Any objections?". Frank starts laughing waiting for an expected approval. He receives no answer then continues, "Interesting. I changed my mind. No, you won't.".

Frank makes waste of him as quickly as he did Barcan. He orders the death of all his most senior commanders he holds responsible for failure. Matilda and her sisters carry out his orders along with the subordinate officers. Most leaders take no joy in this act, but feel they have no alternative. Few look forward to the responsibility of commanding in Frank's army. Their notion is confirmed, it is their life that is owed in failure. Others see an opportunity to showcase their ruthlessness. Yet others a way to replace Frank. It is the why that provokes them to act. Frank calls on his freshly promoted leaders to follow and gather around him, away from the gory scene.

Frank introduces himself to their new responsibilities, "Well, that got out of hand did it not? The energy spent getting this army back in order turns my nose. It attracts a bad energy I care not to experience. It drains my peaceful soul. I take no personal pleasure doing that. But it is a necessary part of enforcing discipline and motivation throughout the ranks. You all do understand that failure is not tolerated. Ever.". Frank's train of thought is brought to a halt. He immediately addresses his senses, "What is that stink? Did one of you savages just decide on their own that we needed to sample their insides? Ok rule number one. If you are experiencing a digestive situation. Warn the rest of us please. It's a common courtesy I would think. I really needed to address that did I? Unbelievable. Here's another rule. Bath yourself at the end of the night. Oh, and gargle water in the morning, I don't want to sample any other body part of yours, especially the one that breaths in my face."

Frank goes on, "Now we have a lot to accomplish in a short period of time. We need our scout teams out there. We need to find out what the situation is. Who is where? What is who doing? Where is who doing what? When is who doing what and where is who going? Why is who, doing what who is doing? How is who doing what, and how is who going where? Did you all get that? Are we all tracking?". Everyone looks around at each other completely confused except for one. Commander Grool answers "Yes, Sir. You want to know everything. Loud and clear.". Frank, pointing at Grool, says with excitement," THANK YOU! So nice to have an understanding. I'm going to go take it down and rest for a few. I need to recharge and focus on what's next. If no-one has anything else for me. This meeting is adjourned. Oh, I must go say hi to my newest sloth buddy. I wonder if he has any insight on our future endeavors. I'm quite sure he does. It's getting the information out of him. He probably misses me. Not probably. I know he does!". Frank leaves the briefing and snickers as he can hear Grool taking charge and organizing the rest of the newly promoted, "I'm not going to lose my head because you idiots...". Frank makes his way over to where he has the only sloth left survived by his army's attack, in captivity.

With Matilda closely behind and his praetorian guards clearing the way, Frank verbally corrects the behaviors of those he sees lower than him. After maneuvering through all the recently battered army warriors, he arrives at a cage that houses a sole augur. He hangs upside down chewing on leaves and twigs. He remains silent staring at Frank and his escorts. Om says nothing. He never does. Om only speaks when he's words are assured and accurate. Yet his prognostications are always ambiguous to the receiver.

Frank says, "Are the accommodations to your liking? I have graciously provided plenty of sustenance and I would think, adequate living conditions have I not? Nasty business it was, the slaughtering of your kind. I understand your position of distain, but please understand. I have a mission to accomplish, and my soldiers know that. They get a little bit, fanatical when I promote a sense of urgency to the situation. You understand that?". Om chews on his latest provided meal. Frank says" You don't want to talk? Okay. I would tell you that at some point your insistence of not cooperating does force my hand to a behavior that is detrimental to your health, and I am losing patience.". Om Yawns. Offended Frank asks, "I bore you, eh? It's ok. Well, I only really want to know the outcome of this most hampered and maddening war." Om continues to stare but says nothing. Frank says, "Nothing huh? You're running out of time. I'll go and take my leave to rest. We'll try again tomorrow. Just know that my tactics to squeeze information out of you will be less then lethal force.". Om finally gives a prophecy, "You will stand alone. Surrounded with nothing or no-one left to kill. You will live long.". Frank smiles with confidence. He feels assured his future is favorable. He retires for the night with a sense of accomplishment. Thanani, Thorn, Gur, Cajole, Roderick, and Goble agree, since Boris is a neutral party, that he should lead and have the final word on this kill expedition. With him, are a flock of owls, hand-picked to help in escorting and protection. Each element of the team members has their own hand-picked guards to assist in this makeshift assault platoon. The Big Horns, Perseus' own and 50 raccoons stand ready and excited. Their mission is to seek out Frank and instill a psychological fear in him and his forces. Boris has sent out a recon team to locate and report all the intelligence needed. And so, the hunt begins. As they approach Frank's main camp sight, Roderick and Gur execute, by way of claws and jaws, all lookouts or sentry soldiers posted as an early alert warning. Boris' escorts do the same. Some ally raptors are left behind to replace those they eliminated. They are meant to mislead the enemy into thinking all is normal. As well as a surprise attack force if need be. Making their way into the edge of a covered tree line darkness helps keep their position undetected. They can observe Frank's army in a state of complacency and vulnerability. They pause to plot their next moves. Roderick still angered and overly aggressive says, "I say we rush down there and start fucking some shit up!". Gur agrees, "Yes, extreme hate and discontent would be an issued order. Thorn, not to be left out adds, "Lead the way gentlemen.". Thanani calms them down, "I understand your passion, but to rush down there like a pack of unorganized berserkers would be reckless and unwise. Patience and controlling your emotions are more important now than ever. Any mistake or underestimation of our situation could lead to our demise.". Cajole says, "I agree.". Gobles point out," Look there! While you three babbles about revenge, do you see?". Cajole says "Cages! There appears to be prisoners or possibly hostages?". Boris says, "Interesting. Now how do you suppose we can use that to further our advantage. Looks to be at least two hundred of them. We must make it a priority to free them. Their release, along with the raccoon's guerrilla warfare, will give us a nice distraction so the focus will not be solely on our assault. My raptors will initiate the tactics from above. The speed and cover of darkness allows the most effect execution. We will send half of our forces to support in this effort. Meanwhile, as it all unfolds and panic sets in; The rest of us will put in motion the main assault. Killing anything that just looks important. Taking advantage of targets of opportunity. If we see Frank and are able to eliminate him. That'll end this whole war. The fog of war will dictate when we disengage the assault. Thanani adds," Certainly, I cannot tell anyone here how to respond to any situation that we may encounter; I will say however, if we are to survive it is of the upmost importance, that we throw our egos away, stay together, and listen to changing events. We really need to support each other. Roderick replies, "If that was directed at me, I take no offense.".

Boris continues, "She's correct. Dying here is not the objective. It is to instill fear and doubt. One last thing. Stay clear of those elephants. It'll take too much effort and it's the quickest way to attend the afterlife.". Boris recalls all his support units and briefs them on the upcoming assault. They coordinate their plan with Cajole and his most ferocious fox warriors. The raptors begin the attack to release the captives from above. Closely followed by the foxes and raccoon as a ground force, preventing anyone from stopping them. The chaos consumes the camps member's attention. They react unprepared. All the captives run to escape or fight for their lives from those that would put them back into chains. The raptors strike with intent to kill. Cajole and his warriors help those that would be restrained. Killing or distracting. They retreat long enough to safely return to the fight. Bandit's elite chosen raccoons go to work causing mayhem. Starting fires, stealing weapons that are needed, and ambushing the enemy from behind. More of Frank's army responds as words get out. Boris and Cajole feel that they are being overwhelmed.

The second assault commences. Roderick and Gur lead the charge shoulder to shoulder. Thanani keeps stride to Roderick's left providing protection and support. Thorn is on Gur's right flank. Gobles follows and acts as a rearguard. All their fellow warriors run along each other's sides at the tip of the spear. They provide an outer kill perimeter to any unlucky challenger. While ongoing close quarter fighting engulfs the scene. All parties involved display self-sacrifice for each other. Putting themselves in harm's way for one another. Gur dispatches those that would do ill harm to Roderick. Roderick without hesitation slays he who would eliminate Goble. Goble put himself in between enemy forces that would end the life of Boris. This show of comradery is repeated over and over again. Frank gets wind of the ongoing disaster. He responds by mounting on top of Matilda and orders her monarch of elephants to form a wall formation. He gathers his praetorian guard to position themselves in a defense posture around the elephants. Short sword at the ready, they slowly press forward. Ambitious raptors and ground forces naively meet their death attempting to take Frank and his companions' life. Matilda and her support, finish off any suspected of still living. She stomps and trumpets her way bloody way forward leading her kind and the others into battle. With Frank mounted securely on Matilda and issuing out orders for a counterattack, he begins to get the upper hand. Slaughtering the escapees and all contesters he sees as the agitators responsible for the main assault. He redirects his platoon to head toward the the main fighting squabble. Boris is drawn to the event. He responds by gaining Roderick and Gur's attention and urges them to withdraw. They Both have other ideas. They aggressively match Frank's intentions to close the distance between them. The dedication of the others invigorates them to support and honor their word to fight for each other. Both sides slash, stab, claw, and bite their way closer to one another. For everyone else, the battle scene is paused while they witness the two sides mangle each other apart. Adrenaline, hate, and revenge, prolong the engagement. Roderick and Gur make a slight breakthrough only to be met with Matilda's stomping feet. They both dodge her tusks and kicking legs. Frank has a difficult time staying mounted on top of her. He attempts to stab at them while holding on. He knows falling off will be his end. The other members of Frank's forces are preoccupied with their own challenges. Roderick loses his balance tripping over a fallen warrior while sidestepping one of Matilda's head swings. As she sees the opportunity to kill Roderick with a crushing head stomp. Boris sinks his talons deep into one of her eyes causing her to fall backward, losing balance, and toppling over. Frank is catapulted off her and into a watery muck. Thorn takes advantage of the situation and goes for Matilda's throat. Following his lead, Thanani, Gur and their warriors jump on her for the death blow. Goble plants his sword deep into her neck. Frank retreats behind his rear-guard and orders and all-out assault. Within seconds reinforcements charge toward Boris and the others.

Boris warns the others, "WE MUST GO! NOW!". The screeching of all the birds alerts all to fallback. They quickly form close together and make their way out of the theater of battle and back to the tree line. Some would be heroes, pursue glory, only to be met with an untimely death. They muster with excitement staying alert for stragglers both friendly and combatants. Gathering their breaths and thoughts, all are ready to reignite the fight. Reason sets in. They form a tactical retreat formation with the raptors providing overwatch to begin their journey back to the refuge. Frank, disheveled and fuming, regroups and heads back to his most concerned casualty, Matilda. She lies dying. He looks down to her in disappointment. Then orders the slaughter of the surviving escapees, all perish except a few. A handful of young elephant bulls that are kin to Matilda and her monarch. Nonparticipant casualties of a war they are unwillingly thrown into. He pushes them close to her as she takes her final gasping breath. Frank looks on as they watch and hear her last heartbeat thump. She dies staring at her offspring.

Frank begins his mind games, "Do you see what they did to your mother? Do you see the cowardly act these savages perpetrated against you? Against us? She must be avenged. You need to answer this most tragic insult. I will make you strong. You will be the sharpened edged sword vengeance. I will lead my army behind your rage so that she may rest is peace.". Frank turns to face his army as they all gather around Matilda and her sons in respect. They all understand the magnitude of the situation.

Frank continues," Behind these young bulls a new and even more powerful army will be built. The savages that attacked us tonight have no idea the shit storm that will be raining on their heads. Soon enough the loss of this great warrior is felt by all. I know this none more than myself. Now more than ever, we must ensure that our resolve is strengthened for our young bulls here. There is much to be a done before payback is served. I trust that you all will rededicate yourselves to our cause, to these young bull's revenge, to your very own lives. We will mourn till the next full moon. We will call to our brothers and sisters. We will train. Then we will fight. WHERE THE FUCK IS GROOL? GROOOOL!". Grool shows himself, "Here sir.". Frank orders him to send word for reinforcements, "Summon them all. Tell them they must honor the call to arms.".

A lone owl discreetly watches everything unfold, knowing that a lethal weapon has been forged and added to an already terrifying war machine. With a purpose they will be on the march. He has no definite answer whether the situation is better or worse. He exits the enemy camp with concerning information. Frank makes his way back to the confinement where he imprisons Om. He hangs from a branch, eating grapes provided to him as a persuasion to cooperate. Frank walks in with purpose toward him clearly irate to witnesses. He slaps the grapes out of Om's hand and stares into his eyes. Frank paces around Om while gathering his next thoughts. Frank says," You knew this was going to happen, didn't you? You knew, and you said nothing. I ask myself. Why do I have you around if you give no information that I may find useful? Om replies, "You will stand alone. Surrounded with nothing or no-one left to kill. You will live long.". Frank remembers, "Ah yes! There is that. But what does that mean? I grow tired of this charade.".

Frank suddenly, and without hesitation, grabs Om by the arm and rips him off the branch. Frank barely struggles holding Om to the ground while unsheathing a Xiphos. In one clean, precise swing of the weapon. He removes Om's head from his body.

Frank's final conversation with Om ends, "I wonder if you saw that coming.".

Book 2 Preview

Grand Owl Boris-

It's been centuries since Dr. P Brocknor's curiosity sparked into action what would come to be known as "The Great Experiment." The successful blending of human DNA with forgotten dogs and cats from local shelters encouraged more aggressive inquiries. Along with the revelation that vampires exist on an ill-fated night. It wasn't very long until the results of their trials evolved and became the source of human demise. These new species learned, grew strong, and turned on their human creators. No longer submissive to their former human masters. They hunted and killed humans until they were believed to be extinct. With no humans left to war with, the new breeds formed their own clans, prides, monarchs, packs, and herds. They settled down and organized. Set up boundaries and traditions. Found deities to worship and then the inevitable. Weres and Vampires went to war. Terriers and Grims, Raptors and Raccoons, Stallions, Rams, and Rhinos fought battles with the big cats who hunted them. Of course, natural alliances formed. Secret pacts were made. Unannounced agendas were hidden away. Now, on the march, is a formidable army ready to destroy them all.

15

BORIS AND THE REST OF THE WARRIORS WHO OPERATED AN ambush, make their escape with minimal casualties. They distanced themselves far enough away to rest and regain their energy and thoughts for the journe. Y back to the wolf refuge. A bon fire is lit. Gur and Roderick go off together to gather food for the rest of the group.

Gur tells Rodrerick, "That was exhilarating! Did you see the look in their eyes when that that mastodon went down?". Roderick replies, "Yea it was. They had no idea what the fuck just shit on their heads. Hilarious! Did you see that weird looking whatever it was that tried to jump on Thanani? Only to get its stomach gutted out. Oh, and the half baboon half Proboscis looking creature? Gur laughing, "Yea!" Roderick continues, "The funny part of that whole deal was, she had ripped his throat out and showed it to him, then shit himself before he hit the ground." Gur laughing out loud, "HAHAHA yea and the others scattered!". Roderick mentions, "Funny. I've been watching her. Now that I time to think about it, Thanani reminds me a lot of Ruby. Her fighting style and movements. They're likeness in size and weight." Gur replies, "I see similarities with those two and Sheeba; except Sheeba is slightly bigger. Besides that, they all do share similar qualities. Ruby's the fiercest. Especially during the blood moon.". Roderick adds, "Sheeba is the strongest and most powerful of the three, but Thanani is the stealthiest." Gur replies, "Agreed. Being who we are. Does it take a genius to figure out that we would have ended up with these life partners? Our destiny would be so much different." Roderick says, "So true. We need strong women like them by our sides."

They spend the rest of the time hunting, tell stories of each other's lifelong love. Laughing and sharing secrets no-one else knows. Sheeba's jealousy of other females, including her sisters. Ruby's obsession with her eye being seen as a weakness. They gather up enough food for the night then head back to the campsite. They return to find everyone already eating.

Thanani tells them, "Took you two long enough. What were you two during?". Gobles suggests, "Probably taking turns dressing up like each other's better halves and having a go." Cajole adds, "Oh! Is that right?" Boris amused joins in "While you two were frolicking around the forest playing tickle the beanbag. Thanani provided us with sustenance via pure blood deer.". Gur replies, "Well lucky you." Roderick dismisses the jokes and assumes, "I guess you won't be wanting any of these squirrels, rabbits, or even this boar.". Thanani replies, "No, No. Bring that boar here. I have a stack of stakes right here to cook that pig with." Roderick says, "Yea, that's what I thought."

Printed in the United States
by Baker & Taylor Publisher Services